ACE, THE BLACK STALLION

Ann Feifel

For Olivia,
My sunshine, and inspiration.

PROLOGUE

It was Friday, the last class of the day. Julia Beemer shuffled in her seat, impatient for the bell to ring. She glanced again at the clock above the classroom door. Fourteen minutes to go. Her English teacher's monotone voice droned on, reading a passage from Shakespeare's play, The Taming of the Shrew. The only shrew on Julia's mind was Casia, Julia's cranky sixteen-year-old chestnut Quarter Horse mare, who might be having her foal this very minute.

Nearing the end of this last pregnancy, Casia had not been her good-natured self. The gentle mare's hostile behavior was abnormal, and it concerned Julia and her father, Martin. The other broodmares had learned to keep their distance from her in the paddock. If they got too close, she pinned her ears, bared her teeth, and lunged at them. Out of character, she'd even pinned her ears at Julia when she brushed her, or entered her stall with a feed bucket. While doing chores, Julia often heard her squeal and kick the walls of her stall. Julia and her father knew it would be a big foal. The poor mare struggled to move around with her massive belly.

Subconsciously, her teacher registered the irritating tic, tic, tic of fingernails on a desk nearby. He stopped mid-sentence, lowered his book, and peered directly at Julia over his wire-framed glasses. Somehow, he knew it was her. Without a word, his raised eyebrows and cold eyes made the point. Heat rose in her cheeks. She clenched her fists and dropped her hands to her lap. The teacher bent his head to resume reading his insufferable book. She sighed and snuck another look at the clock. Thirteen minutes.

***

Julia had grown into an attractive sixteen-year-old. Her fine honey-blonde hair accented her smooth complexion and graceful contours of her face. She was slender and toned from years of horseback riding and helping with chores. Julia's cheery smile and friendly disposition drew people to her, but she kept only a select few horse-crazy girlfriends. Now and then, her warm green eyes reflected a deep shade of melancholy. Only those close to her detected and understood why fleeting moments of sadness crept across her face.

Although Julia was a year older, a group of boys in their sophomore year elbowed each other in the ribs, as she approached in the hallway. Heads turned and eyes followed in unison, as she passed. Crude wolf whistles pierced the air as they admired her tush. Julia pretended not to notice, but their hormone-fueled eagerness brought an amused smile to her face. A few boys from her classes had asked her out on dates. They'd seemed so immature, rambling on about cars, and other topics that she had no interest in. To her, horses were far more fun and appealing than any guy she'd ever met.

Julia had little interest in fashion trends and the latest styles. She preferred comfort, rather than fussing with her appearance. Her makeup case collected dust on her dresser; the contents, a lonely tube of lipstick, one eyeliner pencil, and a stick of blush, still in the wrapper. She gathered her shoulder-length hair into a messy ponytail. Most often, she wore a plain t-shirt tucked into blue jeans, and a comfortable pair of sneakers. The only embellishment to her outfit was an embossed silver buckle on a hand-tooled leather belt that Julia wore with pride. A few years earlier, she'd collected the most points to win the Western Youth Championship at regional riding competitions. At the year's-end banquet, the show committee had presented her with the belt and buckle, along with a gilded trophy with her name engraved.

Julia's school, like every high school in America, had its share of snotty girls who thrived on gossip, insults, and intimidation. They hovered over "their" table in the cafeteria like a pack of wolves, leaning in close to whisper and giggle about their latest victim. The various scents of their perfume permeated the area with an offensive stench. Julia cringed at the sound of their evil giggles. She had no tolerance for bullies. If she overheard them being nasty to another student, she'd step in and stare them down. In fact, Julia presented a challenge for these snobs. They respected Julia for it. Whenever her name arose, they could never seem to dig up any dirty details about her. The only minor faults they could find were Julia's lack of fashion, and that, "Ugh," she often smelled like she lived in a horse barn.

CHAPTER ONE

~Jean and Martin, a new start~

Before Julia was born, her parents, Jean and Martin Beemer, lived in Denver, Colorado. At the time they met, Jean was in her mid-twenties. An avid horsewoman, she had bouncy short blonde hair, a tanned complexion, and an upbeat personality, one who could laugh at anything, including herself. She had a kind and caring heart, especially to animals. Her lively green eyes and warm smile lit up the room when she talked about horses, or other topics she was passionate about.

She and Martin had met one evening in a ballroom, at what Martin's boss from the head office had promised would be a gala event. Instead, it had deflated into a boring flop, soon after waitresses scurried to clear the tables following a tasteless meal.

Single, and nearing thirty, Martin sat at a table with other successful accountants and their partners. Motion at the entrance caught his eye. A striking blonde in a sleek black dress caught a heel and stumbled, but steadied herself on the arm of her date, a colleague of Martin's. He must have cracked a joke about her shoes. She looked down, and Martin could hear the tinkle of her laughter across the room. Martin followed their progress to a nearby table. He kept glancing at her through the meal.

After the meal, Jean's date sat slumped forward in his chair, glassy-eyed and non-verbal. He'd pushed his plate aside and had gulped down almost an entire bottle of wine, leaving Jean to fend for herself, at a table full of strangers.

Unaware she was being watched, she'd collected her clutch and made her way to the bar. Martin's eyes sparkled with amusement at this perky little blonde who sat so unladylike, with her heels hooked over the rung of the barstool, tugging at the hem of her short dress, awkwardly attempting to cover her muscular thighs.

Martin excused himself from his table and wove his way through the crowd towards the bar. "Can I buy you a drink?" he asked.

She turned to the handsome stranger who stood beside her in a tan Armani suit. "No thanks, I was just about to call a taxi," she replied, glancing back with a scowl at the loser she'd arrived with.

"Then I shall sit with you, m'lady, until it arrives," he'd answered, playfully mimicking an English accent. Not in the mood for humor, she responded with a crooked smile, as he slid out the stool beside her.

She couldn't help but notice his angular, clean-shaven face and neatly trimmed brown hair bearing a few wisps of premature gray at his temples. Kind brown eyes, the color of wren's eggs, matched his warm smile, and she caught a pleasant waft of his cologne. He loosened his tie and undid the top button of his shirt.

"There, that's better," he said, as uncomfortable in his suit, as she'd appeared to be in her dress. He stuck out his hand, "Martin Beemer, at your service," he said, once more in his ridiculous accent.

"Jean," she replied, feeling the soft warmth of his hand.

"So, what do you do?" he asked.

"I teach riding lessons to a spoiled group of girls," she replied, and told him a few humorous tales about the stables she taught at.

The closest Martin had been to a horse was when it had trotted past him in a parade. Clueless about the topic, he listened as Jean talked passionately about horses, teaching, and riding.

Suddenly self-conscious, Jean paused when she realized she'd been blabbing on to a complete stranger. The thought crossed her mind that she was more at ease with him, than the pre-sloshed date she'd known for over a month.

"Okay, that's me," she said, "now what about you?"

It was well after midnight when Jean finally called for a taxi. Martin had offered her a ride, but she'd refused. Instead, she reached into his shirt pocket, plucked out his phone and entered her number.

***
~Two Years Later~

Jean and Martin had begun to loathe the hectic city life and detested the confines of their hi-rise condo with marble floors, modern decor, and granite countertops. Floor to ceiling windows provided a panoramic view of the city, but it had given them no pleasure. Their success had come with a price. Neither of them had been happy living in the city. They'd yearned for a quiet place in the country.

The elite equestrian school that Jean taught at was near the outskirts of Denver. Although the job paid well, it was a thankless position teaching spoiled, upper-class students with their fancy riding attire and expensive English tack. Most of them were know-it-all brats. Jean had tolerated their pouty attitudes lesson after lesson, as she repeatedly attempted to correct their riding positions. Her words fell on deaf ears. Half of them were over-horsed with high-priced, hot-headed Thoroughbreds and imported Arabians. Jean knew these well-bred horses had potential, but not in the hands of these hapless riders. She ignored their disrespectful behavior and inattention, but one thing she wouldn't tolerate was if a student was rough or abusive with their mount. Her face white with anger, Jean would quietly take them aside. Through clenched teeth, she'd hiss out a warning… there would be *no* second chance.

Well-paid for her time and service, Jean had dutifully accompanied her students to riding competitions on weekends during the summer. In the practice ring, last-minute instructions failed to improve their chances of leaving the show ring clutching a ribbon. Little good did expensive attire, and high-end tack do them, when they trotted around the show ring blissfully unaware that they were on the wrong diagonal. It infuriated her that these insufferable brats might reflect poorly on her reputation as a well-respected coach.

Many rode from the show ring, dejected and miserable. Twin black lines of mascara mixed with tears trickled down their cheeks. Jean had learned to stand near the exit gate with a pocketful of tissues. She took the heat afterwards, confronted by parents who wondered why their child hadn't placed. They were as arrogant as their darling daughters, and didn't want to hear the truth.

Jean was simply tired of it all.

Martin had worked his way up the ladder with an accounting firm in downtown Denver. He'd attended boring board meetings out of necessity, and sat in his stuffy office at his computer all day, mindlessly opening and closing files for clients. A bottle of aspirin to combat his frequent headaches had sat within arm's reach on his desk.

One evening, after Jean and Martin had silently eaten yet another sodium-laced oriental takeaway, Jean got up, collected the dishes, and tossed the empty cartons into the trash. She walked down the hallway to a closet, pulled out a box, and shuffled through papers until she found what she was looking for, a road map. She unfolded it and spread it across their kitchen table.

They were in a rut, and it was time for a change.

Jean had always wanted her own stables to raise Quarter Horses and teach western riding lessons. Martin just wanted a quiet place where he could learn to raise a few cattle and step out his back door to hear birds chirping, instead of sirens and blaring car horns. They looked over the map, and without hesitation, Jean pointed at Wyoming. They'd driven through there on their honeymoon, and had both loved the mountains, rolling hills and ranch land.

They'd booked a week's holiday and had set off to meet with a sales agent the following weekend. The agent showed them many ranch properties. Some had been too large and expensive, some had poor layouts, and some weren't fit for a mouse to live in.

One by one, they crossed off a list of properties. They began to get discouraged, until mid-week, when the agent had driven along a quiet rural road to a smaller ranch in the foothills near Cody,

Wyoming. He turned down a narrow gravel lane, overgrown with grass and sagebrush, towards the house and stables. Jean and Martin hunched forward in their seats, admiring the mountains far in the distance behind the stables.

As they walked towards the house, the agent lagged behind, as he read the information about the property. He caught up and cautioned them that although the property was within their price range, it had been sitting vacant for five years. The owners had moved out after the bank had taken it over.

The ranch style bungalow was charming on the outside with forest green siding, rustic cream shutters and a thatched roof. Three creaky wooden steps led up to the full-length porch. Wild ivy climbed the hand carved pillars and hung in lacy green tendrils along the roof. Jean pictured the two of them relaxing on the shaded porch on muggy afternoons, while enjoying icy drinks.

As they stepped through the doorway into the house, the first thing that hit them was the musty smell. In the kitchen, a rusted cast iron frying pan sat on the back burner of a filthy electric range. A pot, with the remains of who knows what, sat in an equally filthy sink. Jean wrinkled her nose in disgust and turned away from the dried-up conglomeration in the pot, far beyond recognition. Neither Jean nor Martin dared to open the refrigerator. Two chipped bowls had been left on the kitchen counter beside two matching coffee mugs. The pine cupboards looked decent, other than one door twisted on an angle, held by a single hinge. A clock on the wall read four-thirty-two, the hands forever frozen in time when the battery gave out. A grimy old oak table and four wooden chairs were pushed into a corner near the kitchen window. Jean eyed the set and thoughtfully chewed her lip. Although filthy with grime, and slightly warped in the center, it had character. Rather than heave it out, she envisioned it cleaned and refinished.

She wandered to the kitchen window and glanced down through the hazy glass, at the remains of an old flower bed. She'd never grown a flower in her life, but, she thought, there was the first time for everything. She reached up and drew a heart in the grimy window glass.

The hardwood plank flooring throughout the house uttered a melody of creaks as they walked about. Jean and Martin considered all the scuffs and scratches marring the surface. It would need sanding, and a coat or two of varnish, but it had potential.

The previous owners had either found a deal on paint, or their taste in color coordination was dreadful. The living areas had once been a bright orange, with now filthy, off-white accent walls. The two bedrooms, a brilliant pickle green, brought Jean to wonder how anyone could even sleep in a room that color.

At the stables, wheels screeched along rusted tracks overhead in protest, as the agent tugged the door open. Reaching into the gloom, he located the switch, and two lights flickered on partway down the hallway. Particles of dust glowed in a hazy circle around the lights. From the ceiling, lacy cobwebs sagged with dust, and skeletal remains of insects, long dead. Scattered bits of straw, hay and dried clods of manure littered the hallway as Jean and Martin strolled down it. From what Jean could see in the dim light, the stable was large enough, but the stalls were too small. They would need to bust down walls and change the layout.

Up in the loft, a few bales of moldy hay leaned against a far wall. An old trunk lay open on a pallet. It held musty horse blankets full of holes and droppings, evidence that rodents had enjoyed the run of the place. Cleaned and swept, the loft would be an ideal place to store hay.

To the right of the stables, Jean had walked over to a round pen that appeared newer, and the fencing looked solid. She'd used a round pen to train horses and had found it very useful. They strolled around the paddocks, noting that fencing on two of them needed minor repairs and a fresh coat of paint. In the other two paddocks, countless rails lay on the ground, and entire sections leaned outwards.

They peeked inside a storage shed. If they put up a divider, a small herd of beef cattle could fit in standing stalls on one side, and farm machinery on the other. Jean joked to Martin he'd have to learn to operate a tractor, but with beef cattle, at least he wouldn't have to learn how to milk cows.

A grassy bluff spanned the property across the back. They'd found an old trail and hiked to the top, where they looked across open pastureland and rolling foothills to the mountains beyond. Turning, they'd savored the sight of the ranch spread out below.

Even though they knew it would involve a lot of costly, time-consuming repairs, Martin and Jean had fallen in love with the property. Hand in hand, they'd walked back down to the car where the agent had been patiently waiting. He drove them back to his office and they'd signed their names on the dotted line.

***

By the time Julia was born, three years later, they'd transformed the ranch. The plank flooring gleamed, and they had repainted the walls a warm cinnamon beige. Jean had scrubbed layers of dirt from the table furniture. She'd chosen rustic decorations to match the furniture, and on the walls, she mounted prints with country scenes. In the hallway, she'd hung a hand-painted portrait of herself when she was fourteen, astride her first horse, Ranger.

In the kitchen, she'd put up cheery birdhouse-themed wallpaper, and outside, she weeded and replanted the old flower bed with colorful perennials and tulip bulbs. The saleslady at the country store she'd bought them from, assured her they would be easy to tend. Martin hired a local handyman to help him with the heavy work. Jean had described the changes she wanted done at the stables, and the two men set to work rearranging the layout. Martin, with his smooth city hands, had never swung a hammer except to hang a picture. Before long, blisters formed under his work gloves, as he pulled out boards with a crowbar, and pounded in nails.

They tore down stall dividers, built eight large box stalls along each side, with a combination tack and feed room at midpoint. At the far end, they'd constructed two spacious foaling stalls across from each other. The larger stalls would provide mares and newborn foals with as much comfort and privacy as possible. During the winter, temperatures dipped far below zero in that area of Wyoming, so they re-insulated the outside doors.

They'd repainted and repaired the training ring and paddocks, then built two new paddocks along each side of the lane at the front of the house. Behind the house, away from the other paddocks, they'd erected a high-fenced stallion pen that would also be safe to turn weanlings out in, when the time came.

Martin led Jean up the lane and proudly showed her the new wrought iron sign he and the handyman had hung from the wooden arch across the entrance of their driveway. It read, "Welcome to the Beemer Ranch."

Next, Jean and Martin began Jean's favorite part, their search for broodmares. She'd found out about a ranch that was selling off their stock, so they packed a lunch and drove upstate to go horse shopping. A few days later, a livestock van rumbled down their driveway to deliver a quiet gelding for Martin, and four elegant Quarter Horse brood mares, two in foal. The following day, a truck hauling a livestock trailer delivered eight steers and a load of hay. With the help of a neighbor who owned a large herd of cattle, Martin learned how to feed and tend them. When the farm store called Martin to tell him that his tractor had arrived, he'd grinned like a kid with a new toy, as he drove it down their lane into the yard.

Martin had stood beside Jean outside the stall one evening, thrilled, when their first mare gave birth.

Over time, they'd built a successful Quarter Horse breeding program. Jean hadn't wanted the hassle of owning and handling a stallion and all the extra precautions needed, so they hauled their mares to a stallion upstate.

Horse people in the area had begun taking notice of the quality horses the Beemer Ranch was producing. Jean worked with the foals after weaning, until they were sold. She wistfully watched each horse she'd raised and trained climb onto a trailer, headed off with a new owner.

Jean had also become well known in the area as a top-notch horse trainer and riding coach. They'd bought two quieter geldings and a mare, suitable for lesson horses. Unlike the students at the equestrian center, the students she taught at the ranch were respectful and eager to learn. She smiled at the enthusiasm and progress her students made during each lesson.

At first, Martin was leery around the horses, but over time, he learned how to ride. He'd helped Jean brush and saddle the lesson horses and other horse-related chores around the stables. On quiet evenings when the weather was good, they saddled the horses and explored the hills behind the ranch, or along quiet side roads, stopping to chat with neighbors. On one of their rides, they met Renson Reed, their next-door neighbor, who had walked out his driveway to the mailbox. Renson was a short, wiry man with a leathery face, unshaven, and slightly bow-legged. Jean and Martin had introduced themselves and told him about their horses. Jean asked him if he was married, hoping that he had a pleasant wife to make friends with. He'd given a gruff laugh and told her, "No," in a nasty tone, "I've never been married, and that suits me just fine." They'd talked for a while longer, told him to drop by, then continued on. Jean had looked back to make sure Renson couldn't hear her, and quietly said to Martin, "I don't care for that man. There's just something about him that rubs me the wrong way."

Martin just shrugged the comment off, and thought Jean was too quick to judge people.

One afternoon, Martin had been up in the loft at the stables, making room for a load of hay they'd ordered. Normally, Jean would have helped, but she hadn't been feeling well. Thirsty after working in the hot, dusty loft, Martin went to the house for a lemonade. He carried it out to the porch, where Jean joined him, sitting quietly for a few moments, watching the horses in the front paddock. Normally talkative, Martin cocked his head at her, concerned with her silence. Sensing his eyes on her, with a reserved smile on her face, Jean announced that she was pregnant. Martin jumped up, pulled her up out of her chair and swung her around, thrilled with the wonderful news. The baby was due the following spring.

CHAPTER TWO

~Jean~

Jean had purchased Casia as a weanling shortly after Julia was born. She was a lovely little chestnut filly with a star and snip on her face, and flaxen mane and tail. Jean had worked with many young horses, but she soon realized that Casia had an extraordinary temperament. When Jean trained her to lead, Casia had stepped lightly along beside her with no issues. Her manners were almost faultless. The filly bonded to Jean, trusting her with everything new that Jean introduced her to.

In her second year, Jean lifted a saddle to the filly's nose to sniff. Casia was more concerned about a fly on her flank, than the saddle. When Jean placed it slowly onto her back, Casia turned her head, curious, but not afraid of the strange object. The following summer, when Jean mounted her the first time, Casia danced sideways a few steps, unaccustomed to the weight. She soon settled, and stepped ahead willingly. With only a few short weeks under saddle, Jean was impressed with Casia's smooth gaits and transitions from walk, jog, and lope. Casia became Jean's favorite mount.

***

As a toddler, Julia's mother would prop her up on a barrel beside the ring, while she trained Casia, or taught lessons. Her little face peeked between the fence rails, watching. Martin sat Julia on his knee in the bleachers and watched the "horsies," as Jean and Casia rode past in the show ring. They became a successful team in western riding events and took home many ribbons and trophies.

When Julia was five, Jean buckled a tiny black hardhat onto Julia's head. She wore an all-encompassing smile when Jean lifted her up onto Casia for her first riding lesson.

She showed Julia how to brush the horses, to pick their hooves out, and to be gentle, but firm enough to earn their respect. On a warm day she cross tied one of their quiet geldings in the wash stall outside, and carried out a big soapy pail of warm water. Washing the horse was a fun event for both of them. With a large sponge, Jean scrubbed the horse's back and neck, then handed it to Julia to do the belly, chest, and legs. They were both soaked by the time they hosed him down and dried him with a sweat scraper. Afterwards, at the house, they laughed as they stripped off their wet clothes at the door.

The most important lesson Jean taught Julia was to treat horses with kindness and patience. She described how a mistreated horse would turn sour, and fight back in a raging mass of solid muscle. She explained how they could become easily ruined by heavy-handed riders that continued using the old ways of breaking horses with brute force.

Julia was eight years old the day Jean gathered her beloved daughter into her arms, on the big brown chair in their living room. She held her tight and cried into her Julia's silky hair. Jean had not been feeling well, and had finally gone to see her doctor. After extensive tests, she'd received an ominous call from the doctor's secretary that he needed to see her right away. Jean and Martin stood numb, side by side in his office, as her doctor relayed the terrible news. She had an aggressive, untreatable form of cancer. She passed away shortly after Julia turned nine.

Martin was a happy-go-lucky, kind-hearted family man who adored his wife and daughter. He'd always had a smile on his face. When he lost Jean, grief overcame him. He struggled with trying to manage the stables, and being a single parent, trying to comfort his broken-hearted daughter. One night, weeks later, as he sat in their darkened living room, he considered selling the ranch. The glint of Jean's horse trophies on the shelf above the television caught his eye. She had loved her horses, and had put her heart into the ranch. Julia shared her mother's passion. This was the only home she'd known, and she loved the horses, especially Casia, who had become Julia's mount after her mom had passed away. He couldn't sell the ranch, knowing it would devastate Julia even more.

Father and daughter stumbled miserably through the first few years. Instead of coddling Julia and allowing her to drown in self-pity, he kept her busy with easy chores in the house and around the stables. Julia learned how to make a wicked beef stew and could whip up a hearty breakfast like no one's business. Although she loved being in the stables with the horses, she resented having to muck out stalls and help shovel the cow shed after school. She would have rather plopped down in front of the television and watched The Black Stallion, or re-runs of My Friend Flicka.

Although Martin talked to Julia about her mother and tried his best to cheer her up, it was Casia who had helped Julia through the worst days. Sharing a special bond, Julia had turned to Casia for friendship and solace. The gentle mare had always lowered her head for a sobbing Julia to wrap her arms around her neck. She talked to Casia like she was a person, pouring her heart out. The mare's ears flicked back and forth, listening. Then she'd given Julia a nudge with her muzzle, as if to say, "Okay, that's enough," making Julia smile. Julia kissed the mare's soft muzzle and told her, "Thank you, my sweet girl, you are my bestest friend."

As she grew older, Martin gave Julia more responsibilities. He taught her how to manage most aspects of the ranch, when she wasn't at school, or off trail riding with friends. She learned how to keep the books up to date.

When they set off looking to purchase brood mares or geldings for resale, Julia had her mother's eye for quality horses. She was much better at bartering with potential buyers for a good price, than Martin was. She knew which horse to match up with a beginner, or if someone was looking for a spirited games horse.

On warm evenings after their chores, Julia and Martin often retired to the porch, sinking into soft cushions on two creaky old willow chairs Julia's mother had bought at an auction. Their porch provided first-class seats with a panoramic view of the lowlands and the majestic Bighorn Mountains in the distance, often snow-capped, or shrouded in crystalline clouds. The lowlands held a variety of scenery, with fields of colorful wildflowers, hay crops, and sprawling ranches with lush green pastures. In the foothills, horses, cows, and sheep grazed on grassy slopes, along with deer and elk.

Julia and Martin talked about their days, and ranch-related topics, as darkness crept across the valley and the sun sank behind the mountains. They often heard coyotes yipping in the distance. From the stables came the peaceful sounds of the horses, snorting and shuffling in their stalls as they bedded down for the night.

Now and then, they caught sight of small bands of mustangs that had wandered down from the foothills, to graze. Julia and Martin had heard legends and folklore tales that these scattered bands of wild horses in Wyoming are descendants of Buffalo Bill's horses from his Wild West Show. In fact, they'd been told that they had named the city of Cody after William "Buffalo Bill" Cody.

One day at the feed store, they'd stopped to chat with the salesman. Julia enthusiastically told him about the mustangs they'd seen. The salesman's easy-going smile faded, and his face took on a somber look. He told them that every few years the government of Wyoming hired people to round up the mustangs, to reduce their numbers.

When Julia asked him why, he'd replied, "Cattle ranchers claim these bands consume vast areas of grazing land they need for their livestock. Cattle farming is a big money-making business, and the government stands behind them, unfortunately."

"That's not fair," said Julia. "They deserve to be free. What do they do with them?"

"Well, they release some of them back to the wild, but not many."

"And the others?"

"Luckily, volunteer groups attend the roundups. They take as many horses as possible to temporary ranches and farms, where they advertise, and hope to find homes for them. Sadly, some never get adopted. They live in holding pens. They're fed, watered, and taken care of health-wise, but that's all."

"Is there nothing that people can do to stop the round-ups?"

"Not really. Mustang advocates have tried to fight the laws for years, with petitions and protests, but their words fall on deaf ears when it comes down to money. If it wasn't for the volunteer groups that attend the roundups, I'm afraid they'd all be destroyed."

On the way home, Julia asked her dad if he'd take her to a roundup, but Martin had refused. "It's just not something I want you to see. I know how much it would upset you."

Julia decided that when she was old enough, she would get involved in helping the mustangs.

Martin hadn't told Julia he'd once driven past a round-up. Wondering what was happening, he'd gotten out to watch for a few minutes. His insides grinding, he was sickened to see a frantic mass of mustangs coming in at full gallop, chased into corrals by wranglers on horseback, all terrain vehicles, and helicopters. The exhausted horses had been lathered in sweat, sides heaving. He witnessed fights among stallions forced together into the crowded corrals. Mares and foals, separated in the chaos, called out pitifully for each other. He'd spoken to a veterinarian in attendance. The veterinarian told him he was there to euthanize any badly injured horses.

***

When they had time on weekends, Julia and Martin saddled their horses and went for trail rides up behind the ranch. During one of their rides, Julia mentioned to Martin that she wanted to show Casia. She pleaded her case; she could use her Mom's show saddle and bridle. All she wanted were a few lessons to brush up on her style, and a show outfit for herself. Martin, a pushover for his daughter in most cases, agreed. He hadn't attended a show since Jean had passed away.

Martin lacked any knowledge to prepare Julia for showing. She would need proper riding lessons. He asked his friend at the feed store if he could recommend a riding coach for her.

A kindly middle-aged instructor named Cathy began teaching Julia in the same ring her mother had taught in. Cathy was pleased to find that Julia had a good seat, and already knew the basics of western riding. There were a few corrections she would have to make with her style. She needed to sit up taller in the saddle, keep her heels down, legs snug to the mare's sides, and look ahead to where she was going.

One day as Julia brushed Casia before her lesson, Cathy walked into the stable carrying an English saddle, bridle, and hard hat. Julia eyed the small saddle and shook her head at Cathy. Cathy placed the saddle on the rack, jokingly popped Julia's western hat off into the air and replaced it with the hard hat. Julia turned her back, her face scrunched into a frown as she buckled it under her chin. It was uncomfortable, but Julia forced a smile when Cathy raised her eyebrows at her.

Casia accepted the English saddle and bridle with no problems. The saddle didn't feel much different, and she was used to a thick snaffle bit in her mouth. When Julia climbed into the saddle, it felt like a hard, slippery, chair. She was used to the padded suede seat of her western saddle. The shortened stirrups put Julia's legs into a strange position. How odd it felt to grip the reins in two hands instead of one, with her thumbs placed on top of the braided reins. Rising to the trot was harder than it looked, and it had surprised Julia that after an hour's lesson, her calves ached.

Cathy left the saddle and bridle at the ranch, and encouraged Julia to practice between lessons. She strongly suggested that it would be beneficial for Julia to learn the basics of English riding. After yet another English lesson a few weeks later, Julia led Casia back to the stables. She removed the English saddle and brushed past Cathy to place it on the rack. She'd been unusually quiet through the lesson, and Cathy stared at Julia's back, wondering what was going on. When Julia tried to dart past Cathy with a brush in her hand, Cathy cut her off and stood her ground.

"Okay, Julia, what's going on?"

"I'm sorry, Cathy," Julia said, her head hanging, unable to meet Cathy's eyes, "but I want to show in western classes. I prefer western, and I have my Mom's show saddle and bridle to use. Besides, you know Casia's slow and steady gait is better for western riding."

"Fair enough, Julia. At least you know most of the basics for English. Some day you might change your mind."

Julia was back in her western saddle the following week, but Cathy wasn't easy on her... "You're letting Casia's front end drop, I want to see a smoother lead change, you're not sitting deep in your seat," and so on. She chided her for every minor mistake, but Julia didn't mind. She wanted to be as good a rider as her mom had been.

Nearing the end of the summer, Cathy told Julia she should be ready by mid-September to attend the last competition of the season. Excited with the news, Julia gave Casia a hug. "We're going to a show, Casia!"

On the show morning, Julia was up before daylight. While Martin showered, she fed the horses, then led Casia to the wash stall and bathed her. She toweled the mare dry, then buckled on a light blanket to keep her clean. She applied hoof shine to the mare's feet. When Martin walked into the stables with a cup of coffee in his hand, he chuckled. There sat Julia, cross-legged on a blanket in the hallway near the mare's stall, oiling and polishing her Mom's show saddle and bridle. Martin helped Julia wrap Casia's legs with protective bandages before they loaded her into the horse trailer.

Julia took home a yellow ribbon, placing third in a novice class. She talked his ear off all the way home. Her smiles and enthusiasm were all worth it. Martin was happy that Julia had finally found an enjoyable sport to focus on, after losing her mother.

The following summer, it wasn't long before Julia and Casia became a successful team on the local show circuit. They took home many first and second ribbons, and even won small cash prizes. Julia rearranged the shelf with her mother's trophies, to make room for her own.

At a show near the end of the season, Cathy joined Martin beside the rail, watching Julia ride in a western youth class. As Julia left the ring with a blue ribbon, Cathy remarked to Martin how great the pair were doing. They walked together back to Casia's stall. In the stall, as Julia removed Casia's saddle and bridle, Cathy spoke to Martin with a lowered voice. Julia strained to hear the conversation taking place outside the stall. She overheard Cathy say something about the regional circuit shows the following year. Julia's face lit up. As she carried the saddle and bridle out of the stall, Cathy caught her eye and winked at her.

Martin didn't share her enthusiasm. They good-naturedly argued about it all the way home. Martin wasn't keen about having to travel around the state. Plus, he pointed out, they had a stable full of horses to look after. Who would take care of them?

Julia gradually wore him down. She brought the subject up now and then, through the winter. By springtime, he gave in, and agreed. He knew this is what Jean would have wanted, and gladly done for their daughter. He arranged to pay a neighbor to care for the horses while they were away. He knew the cattle would be fine in the open pastureland above the ranch.

The large Open Western classes at her first regional show intimidated Julia. She was a pre-teen novice, competing in a congested show ring against all age groups, including adults. Julia's stomach churned with nerves. She tensed up and shortened her reins. Casia, unaccustomed to pressure on her mouth, chewed the bit and tossed her head. Whenever a horse passed too close, Casia pinned her ears back, and her eyes flashed in annoyance. The judge's keen eyes took note. They didn't even place in any of the novice or youth classes at that first show.

Many times, during her lessons at home, Cathy had chided her to "look ahead" to where she was going. In the crowded show ring, she began to realize how important it was. She kept watch and circled away from riders clumped up in groups, avoided being forced against the rails or hemmed in on corners. Even in the congested ring of the Open Western classes, Julia gained confidence. Once Julia relaxed the tension on the reins, Casia moved along in fine style, listening to Julia's aids. The team began taking home ribbons even in the large open classes.

At a mid-summer show, Julia committed a grave error that could have ended in disaster. Casia was in her stall during the lunch break. To allow comfort for the mare to eat, Julia slightly loosened the cinch on her saddle. Julia had been chatting with some friends when they'd announced her next class over the loudspeaker. In a rush, she took Casia from her stall and asked Martin to give her a leg up. She'd forgotten about the cinch. In the show ring, they made it through the walk and jog commands without Julia noticing anything amiss. When the judge asked for a lope to the left, one stride later, Julia felt the saddle slip to the right. Mortified, she realized her blunder. She leaned hard to the left and dropped her weight into the left stirrup. Thankfully, that shifted the saddle back into place. Her cheeks burned as she reined Casia into the center of the ring and dismounted. Disgusted with herself, she'd learned a tough lesson.

In the smaller Western Youth Pleasure classes, although the competition was tough, the two became a dynamic team. Casia floated along the rails, showing off. The judges admired the flashy chestnut mare with the flaxen mane and tail. Julia's grueling riding lessons with Cathy had paid off, too. Julia had also won horsemanship classes judged on the rider's style. That year, she'd won the belt and buckle at the year-end awards banquet.

***

Julia and Martin sat on the porch one cool evening in October, wrapped in cozy blankets, watching the stars. They'd talked about Julia's new school, her homework, and how different high school was, compared to middle school. She'd complained to Martin that her teachers must take evil delight in piling homework onto freshmen. Each night after supper, Julia sat at her desk, working on projects and assignments. Most weekends were a bust for anything else but homework.

Julia had surprised Martin that night, when out of nowhere, she'd suggested, "Why don't we breed Casia? I hardly have time to ride anymore, and she'd make beautiful babies."

Martin's eyes searched her face in the pale light shining coming from the window behind them, unsure if she was serious. "Well, she'd definitely make a good broodmare, but that's up to you. She's your horse."

Through the winter, they asked around and did some research on the internet and found a few prospects that sounded promising. In the spring, they'd driven around to various breeding stables to see them in person. They decided upon a solidly built palomino

Quarter Horse stallion, Sir Parker's Dream. He had excellent bloodlines and an impressive show record.

The following spring, Julia and Martin had quietly watched outside the stall as Casia gave birth to a handsome palomino colt, like his sire. They named him Beemer's Golden Dream. Goldie, as they fondly named him, was sold as a two-year-old gelding to a young cowboy looking for a reining prospect.

CHAPTER THREE

~Casia~

Martin and Julia realized that there was a good market for Appendix horses: a cross between a Thoroughbred and an American Quarter Horse. The combination produces the height, refinement, and agility of a Thoroughbred, with the calmer attitude and solid bone structure of a Quarter Horse. Appendix horses were becoming more and more popular for English riding events. With powerful hind quarters and speed, they were also proving desirable as gaming horses.

The stallion they'd chosen to breed Casia with was a tall, sleek, black Thoroughbred, a very handsome horse. In her sixteenth year, she was getting to an age where pregnancy and foaling presented potential risks. They'd decided this would be her last pregnancy. After this foal, she would retire to grassy pastures.

Julia was hoping Casia would have a filly. She wanted another mare like Casia to keep as her own riding horse, although she realized it might not have Casia's personality and temperament. She hoped the foal would be black like its sire, at least. Julia and Martin had decided if Casia produced a fine quality colt, they would keep him to use as a stallion to breed with their other brood mares.

***

The day Julia anxiously waited in class for the bell to ring, Casia had been two weeks overdue.

When they'd fed the horses that morning, Casia had been dripping milk from her udder, showed no interest in eating, and pawed restlessly at her bedding, all signs that labor would begin soon. As they walked back to the house, Julia had asked if she could stay home from school, to be there for the birth. Martin would have no part of it. Julia pleaded with Martin, but he stood his ground, pointing out the fact that she could not afford to miss any classes, since final exams were coming up soon.

As she took a quick shower, Julia clenched her jaw so hard, her teeth hurt. When shampoo dripped down her forehead into her eyes, the pain felt good in a way, to match her anger. After furiously toweling herself off, she yanked on her clothes, grabbed her backpack and lunch off the counter and slammed the outside door loud enough for Martin to hear it. He didn't hear her curse under her breath or see her swipe the hot tears off her cheeks. She flipped her damp hair off her face, and with long angry strides, she stomped up the driveway like a child having a tantrum, her sneakers scuffing up the dust.

Neither of them had any inkling of the tragic events that would unfold later that night.

***

Finally, the school bell rang. Julia swiped the books and papers off the desk into her backpack. At her locker, she was ready to scream as she fumbled with the combination. Finally, the lock clicked open and she grabbed her jacket and the rest of her homework. She slammed the door shut, then joined the bottleneck of students streaming outside to the school buses. She hurried around other students to claim the front seat on the bus so she could hop out quickly at her driveway.

Julia sat on the edge of her seat, her stomach in knots. Behind her, incessant chattering of students making plans for the weekend grated on her nerves. Julia ignored them. The bus, agonizingly slow, finally pulled to a stop at her driveway. She grabbed her backpack and hopped off. Her backpack thumped her shoulder with every stride, as she sprinted to the stables.

She dropped her school bag just inside the door of the stables and breathlessly called out, "Daddy?" Her anger from the morning was long forgotten. "Did she have it?"

Martin popped his head out of a stall from where he was forking manure into a wheelbarrow.

"Nope, no foal on the ground yet," replied Martin in an upbeat voice, but Julia could see the worry lines etched into his face. "She was kicking at the walls again earlier and she's very restless."

After he emptied the wheelbarrow outside, he joined Julia in front of Casia's stall, watching as she picked at her hay. The mare let out a squeal and kicked the wall again. The sound echoed down the hallway.

"C'mon, Casia, hurry and have that foal!" Julia pleaded. "Daddy, do you think she'll foal tonight?"

"Who knows, honey, but she's been dripping milk all day, so I think tonight will be the night. I called Vince to make sure he'll be around, just in case she has trouble foaling." Vince was their veterinarian, and longtime friend of Martin's.

Martin glanced sideways at his beautiful daughter as she absently tucked a loose strand of hair behind her ear. He was glad that to see the stiff set of her jaw and the fiery look in her eyes had disappeared. She reminded him so much of Jean. He chucked to himself, realizing his daughter had a temper just like her mother.

They watched the mare for a few more moments, then fed the horses early, in case things got hectic with Casia later. Martin picked up Julia's backpack as they headed out the door. Like she'd done all her life, Julia grabbed her dad's hand, and they walked to the house for supper. Martin heated a can of soup and made sandwiches, as Julia washed and changed out of her school clothes.

After supper, they went into the living room and turned on the television, but neither of them paid much attention to it. Both kept glancing at the monitor connected to the webcam mounted in the foaling stall. At one point, Casia had been picking at her hay but suddenly stopped chewing, pinned her ears back, then turned and bit at her flanks. The restless mare circled her stall. Around ten o'clock, she began lying down, then getting back up. Finally, around midnight, Martin saw her lift her tail, then they both heard a long groan through the sound system.

"Well, I think things are finally happening." said Martin. They took their jackets from the hooks beside the door, Martin flicked on the yard lights, and the two of them headed back to the stables.

They treaded softly down the hallway to Casia's stall, so they wouldn't disturb the mare. A few horses nickered as they passed, hopeful for a treat. Casia was lying on her side, groaning as she strained with a contraction. When it was over, she gathered her legs beneath her and got back up. They watched as she laid down and got back up, again and again. Having contractions every couple of minutes, Casia's neck and chest were soon soaked with sweat.

An hour later, there was still no sign of the foal. Martin decided it was time to call Vince. He answered on the second ring.

"Hi, Vince, it's Martin. I think you'd better come. Casia has been in labor for an hour, now, and nothing is happening."

"On my way!" replied Vince, and he was in his vehicle within moments.

Vince kept a well-stocked assortment of medical supplies in his truck. Like all livestock veterinarians, being prepared for medical emergencies is crucial.

Restless with worry, Julia aggressively swept the hallway while they waited for Vince to arrive. This was the first time they'd ever had a mare with foaling problems, and she agonized that it was Casia.

Ten minutes later, they heard Vince's vehicle pull in beside the stables. Vince, nearing forty, with a clean-cut, boyish face, usually wore a jovial smile. That night, as he strode down the hallway towards them, he greeted them with a somber nod. He peered down at Casia, who lay in the straw, her sides heaving.

Vince absentmindedly rubbed a faded scar on his left cheek. It was an old injury, caused by a frightened horse that had shoved him into the metal edge of a stall door.

Vince removed his jacket, got his stethoscope out of his case, then stepped into the mare's stall. He fondly gave Casia a pat on the neck. He'd known her since she was a weanling. He placed his stethoscope on the mare's damp chest and listened. His face creased with concern, when he heard a quick heartbeat. Back in the hallway, he removed an obstetric latex glove from a package in his case. He pulled on the long glove that reached almost to his shoulder. Vince knelt behind Casia, to examine her internally. He gently eased his hand into the birth canal, hoping to feel the two front hooves with the muzzle resting on the legs.

It seemed forever before Vince described the situation to them. "I can feel the hooves, but the neck is bent around, and the head is facing backwards."

They all knew that in such a position, a foal could never pass through the birth canal.

Grunting with the effort, his arm deep inside the mare, Vince explained, "I'm trying to move its head around into place. I can get my fingers around the muzzle, but it keeps slipping out of my grasp."

Five minutes later, he had still not had any luck. Vince and Casia were both soaked with sweat. The situation was critical.

Vince knew that if he couldn't move the foal's head into the correct position soon, Casia and the foal would both die.

Vince withdrew his arm, then said, "Marty, there's a tube of sanitizer in my case. I want you to sterilize your hands. In the left slot of my case, you'll find a Ziplock bag with scissors, and a roll of thin rope in it. I want you to cut me a five-foot length."

Vince took the rope from Martin, tied a loop, and pulled the end through to make a noose.

I hope this works, Vince thought to himself as he guided the noose into the birth canal. Past the tiny hooves and along the legs, he followed the foal's neck and jawline to the muzzle. It was no minor feat getting the noose around the foal's muzzle by feel alone, but luck was on his side, and he got it on the second try. As he withdrew his gloved hand, he kept tension on the rope with his free hand. Just then, the mare groaned and lowered her head into the straw as another contraction hit her. Vince sat down in the straw behind her, bracing his feet against her rump. He gave the rope a steady pull. Inch by inch, he gathered the excess into his hands. Suddenly he lost the tension, and the rope slid out into the straw. Fearing it had slipped off the foal's muzzle, he inserted his hand back into the mare, to check. Within moments, his fingers touched the foal's muzzle, in the correct position.

"I've got it now," he reported, with relief in his voice. "The foal's head was sure stuck tight in there."

The birth proceeded quickly after that. Tiny hooves and forelegs soon appeared, with the muzzle following. Casia pushed a few more times, and a big black colt slid out into the bedding. Casia looked back at her foal and nickered softly. Exhausted, she laid her head into the straw.

Vince kneeled down, tore the afterbirth from the foal's head, and cleared the mucus from his nostrils, but the lifeless colt wasn't breathing.

"Marty, hand me a towel!" Vince called out in alarm and sprang into action. He removed the rest of the afterbirth and briskly rubbed the foal's body with the towel to stimulate his breathing. Finally, the colt's head twitched, his eyes flickered open, and he sucked in his first breath of air.

Julia had been so afraid that the foal was dead, she hadn't noticed if it was a filly or a colt. She was just happy it was alive. When the colt lifted his head, her eyes widened at the unique white blaze on his forehead, in the shape of a spade.

Satisfied that the colt was breathing on his own, Vince turned his attention to Casia.

Mares are usually very attentive to their newborn foals, but Casia showed little interest in it. A few times she raised her head and nickered towards him, but weakly lowered her head back into the hay. Although she'd had a hard labor and had just given birth, Vince had an uneasy feeling that something was wrong. He placed his stethoscope to her damp chest and was alarmed to find her heartbeat had increased. He squatted beside her head and lifted her top lip with his thumb. The mare's gums and tongue were white. Vince had seen other older mares with these symptoms after delivering a foal. He drew in a ragged breath, reluctant to tell Julia and Martin what he feared. Casia may have ruptured a uterine artery.

When the walls of the arteries in the uterus weaken with age, it can be a potentially deadly complication of pregnancy and foaling. One or more of these arteries can rupture. Often, there is no initial sign to indicate internal bleeding. If it is a major rupture, a veterinarian cannot staunch the flow of blood.

"I want to get Casia to her feet," Vince said to them. At first, he didn't tell them what he feared was wrong, and silently hoped getting her up would miraculously help. He gathered the gangly colt in his arms and laid him safely in a corner of the stall. Casia gave a half-hearted attempt to rise when Vince tugged on her halter. She had no strength and lay back into the bedding. Martin went in, and it took both of them pulling and pushing to get her up. She stood trembling, unsteady on her feet, her breathing shallow and labored.

Vince checked Casia's vitals again, dismayed to find no change. Her heart rate still raced, and gums were deathly white.

Within minutes, she began staggering, disoriented, and unaware of her surroundings. The mare had gone into shock.

The men locked eyes. Martin didn't need to hear the words. The mare was dying, and there was nothing Vince could do.

Vince glanced at Julia, her face pressed anxiously to the bars, desperately looking between him and Casia. He dreaded having to tell her the awful news.

Her eyes brimmed with tears as Vince gently shook his head and said, "I'm so sorry, honey, but we have to put Casia out of her misery. A blood vessel has burst inside her, and she's bleeding internally. There's nothing I can do to save her."

"Oh no, no, no!" Julia cried, tears streaming down her face. She went in and softly stroked her beloved mare's neck. "Oh, my poor Casia. I'm so sorry, baby. You've been my best friend, and the best horse, ever." She kissed the mare's velvet nose, then turned to leave. Martin reached out to give her a hug, but she pulled out of his arms and bolted up the hallway out of the stables.

First, she'd lost her mother, and now her beloved mare. In her room, sobbing uncontrollably, Julia mindlessly dropped her clothes on the floor and put on her pajamas. In the bathroom, she pressed a cold washcloth to her face. After climbing into bed, she hugged her pillow, but how she wished for a hug from her mom. Julia lifted her head from the pillow, and through blurry eyes, she looked across at the two-tiered shelf on the far wall. Two of her favorite glass horse figurines sat among the array of trophies she and her mother had won at horse shows. Her eyes moved to rest upon the photo of her mother astride Casia in her show outfit, posing for a professional photographer. She looked stunning in an aqua blue shirt with fringes and matching suede chaps. The brim of her brushed felt hat sat stylishly low across her forehead. Casia stood like a bronze statue, her flaxen mane and tail curved slightly with the lift of a soft breeze. The silver buckles on Jean's show saddle and bridle gleamed under the photographer's lights.

Fresh tears rolled down Julia's cheeks, and dripped off her chin onto her pajama top. She tried not to think about what was going on in the stables.

***

Right then, the two men were in the stables discussing what to do about the colt.

Vince rubbed at the scar on his cheek, deep in thought. "Even after such a rough start, he's a fine, healthy colt, Marty. You have two choices. I can bring you a case of foal replacement milk from the clinic. You'd have to bottle feed him six times a day until he learns to drink from a bucket. If you can find someone with a mare that's lost a foal, or a mare with a foal that might accept him, that would be much easier. It's too bad none of your other mares have foaled yet."

Before they talked any further, Vince entered Casia's stall and washed her udder, while Martin tried to hold the trembling mare steady. He took a nursing bottle from his case, then bent down and milked Casia's colostrum from her udder. Colostrum is the early milk a mare produces, rich in vital nutrients for a newborn foal. Vince screwed the nipple onto the bottle, then squeezed a tiny amount of milk into his hand and held it to the colt's quivering muzzle. The colt picked up the scent and licked off the milk. Instinctively, he searched around for more, found the nipple that Vince offered him, and sucked the bottle empty.

They helped Casia into the hallway and closed the stall door. At the doorway, Martin flicked a light switch, illuminating the far side of the cattle shed. Outside, the two men gripped both sides of her halter and steadied the mare as she stumbled along between them. They led her past the cattle shed to an open grassy area, where Vince put her out of her misery.

As they walked back to the stables, Martin sighed, "I have a hole to dig, but first I'll call Renson, next door. I ran into him yesterday, and he told me one of his mares had foaled two weeks ago. Maybe she'll accept the colt."

They looked in on the colt, then Martin placed a call to Renson. He realized that at four in the morning, Renson would be still sleeping, but under the circumstances, he thought he'd understand.

CHAPTER FOUR

~A surrogate family~

The phone rang four times before Renson's sleepy voice answered with a raspy, "Hello?"

"Hi, Renson, it's Martin. Sorry to wake you up, but we lost a mare who foaled a short time ago. She ruptured a uterine artery, and we had to put her down. Her colt is doing fine, but I wonder if you have any nursing mares that might accept him?" he asked, then added, "I'd rather not have to bottle feed him."

Renson rubbed his eyes and tried to clear his head to think for a moment.

"Sorry to hear about your mare, Martin." he said. "I have one mare that might accept him. She has a two-week-old filly. She accepted an orphaned colt a few years back, when her own foal died. Bring him over and we'll see what happens."

Martin peeked in at the colt, then went to the house to look in on Julia. He was glad to see she was asleep. He left her a note on the table, grabbed his keys off the hook, and locked the door behind him.

Vince was just putting his medical case into his truck. Together, they loaded the frightened colt into the cargo hold of Martin's jeep.

Weary and cold, Vince got into his truck, looking forward to climbing into a warm bed. He rolled down the window and said, "Good luck with the colt, Marty! Let me know how things go at Renson's. We'll square up later."

***

Renson was walking to his stables as Martin pulled in. Martin backed his jeep up to the stable door to unload the colt. When he lifted the hatchback, it startled the colt, and his long legs scrambled for a foothold.

"Wow, what a fine big colt, Martin, and look at that marking on his forehead!" exclaimed Renson.

"I just hope Jasmine will accept him," said Renson.

"Ya, you and me both."

The newcomer in the stables caused a ruckus of whinnies and nickers from Renson's horses as the men carried the struggling young horse up the hallway towards Jasmine's stall.

Jasmine and her two-week-old filly, Fauxy Lady, were both sorrel chestnuts. The broodmare was a flashy Quarter Horse with a flaxen mane, a small white star on her forehead, and a white sock on one of her forelegs. Jasmine, like all Renson's horses, had Renson's double **RR** branded on her rump.

Fauxy Lady had a fine, tapered head with a star and snip on her face, and two white socks on her forelegs.

In the event that the mare might turn on him, Martin used a safe method of introducing the colt to Jasmine. He lifted the colt up to Jasmine outside the stall. Her ears perked forward as she sniffed curiously at him through the bars.

The men waited as the mare drew in his scent, then her muzzle quivered as she gave a soft nicker.

"Well, that sounds hopeful." said Martin. Renson nodded in agreement.

Renson slid her stall door open, and Martin lowered the newborn colt down just inside the open doorway of the stall, ready to pull the colt out of harm's way, if Jasmine rejected him. The mare could lash out at him with her front hooves.

Jasmine turned to check on her filly, Fauxy Lady, who was shyly hiding behind her. The mare sniffed at the colt and nickered again, then gave him a gentle nudge. Nothing in her manner suggested any hostility. Encouraged by her nudge, the colt struggled to arise.

Renson stepped around the colt, and held Jasmine by her halter off to the side of the stall, providing more room for the colt, as he thrashed around in his first attempts to rise. He extended his front legs, but his back end wouldn't cooperate. The colt wobbled sideways, collapsing against the wall. On the next try, he made it up partway, but lost his balance, tipped over onto his nose, and fell forward. Again, and again, he attempted to gain his footing. It was an amusing sight for the two men, and they chuckled, knowing from experience that this was normal for newborn foals.

Finally, on his feet with his four legs splayed out front and back, the colt stood, weaving, trying to keep his balance. He attempted to take a step but teetered sideways, and collapsed into the straw. Determined, he repeated the process again, before he successfully took his first wobbly steps towards the mare.

Foals are born with an instinct to nurse as soon as possible. This hungry colt was on a mission. Looking for milk, he searched Jasmine's chest. Renson released her head, to bond with the colt. When she softly probed his quivering muzzle, he emitted a nicker of delight. She nickered back, and tenderly nudged him towards her udder. The colt could smell her milk, and nosed along her belly to find the source. When he located her udder, the men could hear him sucking greedily. His little black tail swished back and forth with pleasure.

Through all this, Fauxy Lady remained behind Jasmine, but finally poked her head out to look at the colt. Not sure what to make of him, she cautiously sniffed at him as he suckled, then retreated to a far corner, to lie down.

Jasmine turned, and nudged the colt's rump again. Satisfied the colt was no threat, she reached down for a mouthful of hay.

"What a sweet little filly you have there, Renson," exclaimed Martin as he looked at Fauxy's refined head. "She's got beautiful markings."

"Isn't she?" said Renson. "I bred Jasmine to a stallion over in Bear Creek. I'm pretty pleased with the way her filly turned out. I should be able to get a good buck for her, after I put some training on her. I'm hoping she'll be a good Western Pleasure horse like her mother was. Jasmine did great in Western Pleasure classes, but she popped a rear tendon. I rubbed it with liniment and wrapped it, but the darned thing never healed properly. Since I couldn't sell her as a riding horse, I decided I'd use her as a broodmare."

***

What Renson didn't tell Martin, was how Jasmine had popped the tendon. Renson had a short fuse when he got angry. One day, when he climbed into the saddle for a ride, Jasmine was full of energy, and acting fidgety. When he asked her to jog, she broke into a lope, instead. He yanked on the reins with brutal force. The curb bit hit the roof of her mouth, and the mare stopped dead from the pain. Renson jabbed her with his spurs, forcing her into a hard spin, round and round on the spot. Dizzy, she stumbled in the sand, her rear leg twisted, and the tendon ruptured. The poor mare hopped back to the stables on three legs. It was weeks before the swelling went down.

As they walked out of the stables, Martin thanked Renson, telling him he'd be back later in the day to check on the colt. Dead tired, Martin headed home. He fed the horses, headed to the house, and crawled into bed to catch a couple of hours sleep.

CHAPTER FIVE

~Ace, Jasmine and Fauxy Lady~

Julia slept fitfully. Every time she rolled over, she woke up thinking about Casia. As the first rays of light peeked through her curtains, she finally fell into a deep sleep. It was almost eleven when Julia woke to the sound of her dad's tractor running. When she realized that he was burying Casia, all the horrible events came crashing back. She buried her face in her pillow, and wished it was all a horrible dream. She closed her eyes and thought about staying in bed all day. Her eyes popped open. *What about the colt? Was he scared and all alone in Casia's stall? Was he even still alive?*

Julia looked in the bathroom mirror at her blotchy face and puffy eyes, but she didn't care. She showered and got dressed. Martin was making toast and eggs when she walked into the kitchen.

"Hi, Daddy. What happened with the colt last night?" She looked at him questioningly, through bloodshot eyes.

Martin gave Julia a bear hug, then told her about the colt and Renson's mare.

"Can we go see him?" her voice seemed a little brighter as she pulled out a chair at the table.

"Absolutely!" said Martin. He wanted to see the colt as much as she did.

"I've been trying to think of what we should name him. Any ideas?" Martin asked, attempting to keep her mind on the colt, and not Casia.

"Daddy, did you see that white star on his face? It reminds me of an Ace of Spades in a deck of cards." She thought for a moment. "What about Ace? Beemer's Ace of Spades?"

At the stove, he turned to her, smiling. "Funny, I thought the same thing about that star. Beemer's Ace of Spades, it is!" They included Beemer in his name, like every foal born on the Beemer ranch.

As he placed the two plates on the table, Julia sat, staring off into space. It broke Martin's heart to see such sadness on his daughter's face, again.

"He's one nice looking colt, isn't he?" Martin asked, to distract her.

Julia nodded. Her shoulders drooped in misery.

"Listen, honey, remember we decided to breed the other mares to that same Thoroughbred stallion? I promise you, we'll get you a nice filly sooner or later," he added.

Julia picked at her breakfast. She had no appetite and scraped her plate into the garbage. As Martin finished his breakfast, his gaze fell on Jean's abandoned flower bed outside the kitchen window. Julia had half-heartedly tried to tend it, but only a few flowers clung to life amidst the tangle of weeds. His eyes shifted up to the wallpaper Jean had hung. Seams were split and peeling, and the bright colors had faded. Neither Martin nor Julia had the heart to tear it down. In fact, they had changed none of the decor that Jean had lovingly selected.

Martin leaned his elbows on the table, his chin in his hands. He felt so inadequate without Jean. Julia needed the comfort of her mother.

Julia noticed his distress. "Daddy, are you okay?"

He got up with his plate and nodded, not trusting his voice.

After rinsing the dishes, Martin announced, "We'll do the chores first, and then head over to Renson's after that, okay?"

Julia nodded, feeling guilty. She knew her dad was having a rough time, too.

As they walked out to the stables, Julia gripped Martin's hand, afraid to see where he'd buried Casia. She was glad the grave was out of sight. She wanted Martin to make a cross, but she couldn't face seeing the grave yet.

At the doorway of the stables, Martin turned and hugged Julia again. "I'm so sorry, honey. We sure didn't expect this to happen, did we? You know Vince couldn't have saved Casia. We're lucky they didn't both die."

"I know, Daddy, but I'll miss Casia so much," replied Julia, as tears welled up in her eyes once again. She wiped them away with her sleeve, then went to get the wheelbarrow out the back door. She avoided looking into Casia's empty stall as she walked past.

They turned out the horses, mucked out the stalls, and filled the outside water troughs. Julia felt better by the time they got into Martin's jeep. She looked forward to seeing the colt.

Renson was in his stable, brushing one of his horses on crossties when they walked in.

"Hi, Renson, how are things going with the colt?" Martin asked.

"Going well," replied Renson. "Jasmine is doing fine with the two of them. Fauxy tried her best to get that colt to play with her in the stall a while ago. He was laying down, and she pawed at him to get up. She finally gave up and laid down beside him." He chuckled.

The three of them walked to Jasmine's stall and looked in. Both foals were up, nursing on either side of the mare.

"You know that star on his face?" Martin asked Renson. "This morning, Julia and I named him Ace of Spades, Ace for short."

Renson chuckled, replying, "Well, it sure suits him. In all my years, I've never seen a horse with markings like that."

Julia asked Renson if she could go into the stall.

"Sure. Go ahead, Julia. Jasmine is a quiet mare. She'll be fine for you to go in."

Julia entered the stall quietly, and squatted down near the doorway, waiting for the foals to finish nursing.

Much sturdier on his feet now, Ace finished nursing and turned to look at her. Fauxy walked over and stood beside Ace. When Julia extended her hand, they hesitated.

Fauxy, being two weeks older, and used to Renson being in the stall, took the first steps towards Julia. She stretched her neck out to sniff Julia's hand, and decided it was safe. Ace followed her lead, and soon, both foals were enjoying chin scratches. They sniffed at Julia's hair, face, and jacket. She smiled as their long whiskers tickled her face. When Ace nibbled on her chin, Julia giggled. When she gently scratched his neck below his wispy mane, his little muzzle went up into the air, with his newborn, stubby tail flicking in pleasure.

Martin knew that this was the best therapy for Julia after the horrible events of the night before.

Cramped from squatting, Julia stood up and asked Renson, "Can I come back and see them again tomorrow, Mr. Reed?"

"Sure," said Renson, "Just make sure you latch the stall door when you leave."

Of course, I would, thought Julia, irritated that he felt the need to mention it. She'd been around horses and in stables her whole life. Something about Renson's attitude bothered Julia. She really didn't like him.

Some time ago, she'd caught him being nasty with one of his horses. Julia had dropped by his place to borrow some foal mix. She'd tried calling him, but he hadn't answered the phone. When she walked into his stable unannounced, she heard a loud curse from a stall down the hallway. Then she heard a bang, followed by the panicked sound of hooves scrambling for footing. She walked down to see what the commotion was about.

Renson was in a young colt's stall, his hair and shirt dripping wet. The yearling was pressed against a wall, his eyes rolling in fear.

Renson had gone into the stall to fill up the water bucket, and the colt had playfully nipped his arm when he turned his back. Renson furiously swung the bucket around and hit the horse on the rump. The water had splashed out of the bucket, soaking Renson.

Julia attempted to suppress a giggle when he told her what had happened. Instead of joining her in finding the humor of it, he'd turned, kicked the colt in the gut and had curtly asked her what she wanted.

***

Julia rode her bike over to Renson's the next day. Jasmine and the foals were out in the round ring. Julia stood at the fence, entertained by the two young ones as they played.

Jasmine was doing her best to keep watch over them as they dashed across the pen like out-of-control toddlers. The way Ace ran, Julia would have never guessed that he was only a day old. He kicked and bucked, and Fauxy would follow suit. They'd pause for a moment, then off they'd tear to the opposite side of the pen. They ran and played until they both decided they were hungry. After nursing, they laid down in the soft sand near the fence where Jasmine stood eating a flake of hay.

Julia rode over to see the foals almost every day after school. When Ace was two weeks old, Renson turned Jasmine and the two foals out into a large pasture with his other brood mares and foals.

***

School ended for the summer. Every day after Julia and Martin finished the morning chores, if she wasn't busy, Julia visited the foals. Ace and Fauxy got to know the sound of her bike tires on Renson's gravel driveway, and ran to the fence to meet her. They greedily gobbled up the tiny pieces of carrots and apples that she carried in her pockets.

The foals nursed less as summer wore on. Both the foals were eating grass, hay, and a grain mixture of foal mix. They ate the foal mix with gusto, greedily shoving each other away from the foal feeder. They were inseparable. Where one went, the other followed, venturing farther away from Jasmine. Both foals grew bigger and stronger. Even though Ace was two weeks younger, by early August, he was as tall as Fauxy. They'd lost their baby fuzz. Their manes were growing sleek, and their summer coats were shiny and healthy.

As October approached, the days grew shorter, and the nights had a chill in the air. The horses began growing thick coats, in preparation for winter. The Bighorn mountains already had snow on the higher peaks, and heavy frost glittered across the pastures in the mornings.

Weaning time for the foals drew near. Not only would they be taken away from their mother, it would also separate the young colt and filly.

CHAPTER SIX

~Ace and Fauxy Lady, weaning time~

During the last week in October, Julia was at school, the day Renson and Martin stood at the pasture fence watching the horses and discussing how Martin would get Ace home. The foals were like gangly teenagers, naughty and irritating for Jasmine and the other mares.

"I think the easiest way is just walk him home." said Martin. "It isn't far, and it's a pain to hook up the horse trailer for such a short distance. Can you keep the three of them in tomorrow morning, and I'll walk over to get him?" asked Martin.

"Sure," replied Renson, "but I won't be around to help. I've got an appointment in town."

"That's okay, Renson, thanks. I'll be fine. I don't expect any problems." said Martin.

Little did he know...

The next morning, Martin walked Julia to the top of the driveway, and stood with her as she waited for the bus. After he saw her off, he walked over to Renson's with his gloves tucked into his back pocket, and a lead line looped around his shoulder.

The foals were usually already outside at this hour. Unhappy at being kept in the stall, they bounced around and bumped into the Jasmine many times. When they tromped through the last wisps of her hay, she pinned her ears at them.

The two young foals were nipping back and forth at each other when Martin walked up to their stall. They turned when they heard him, and their muzzles peeked out through the bars, waiting expectantly to be let outside.

When Martin slid the stall door open, both foals tried to push past him, eager to get out. Martin blocked them, caught Ace by the halter and snapped the lead line on.

"Whoa there, boy," said Martin, trying to settle the young horse with a calm voice.

He gently pushed Fauxy away from the doorway, quickly pulled Ace out into the hall, and slid the door shut.

When Ace realized Fauxy was still in the stall, his head and tail went up in alarm. He trotted in a tight circle around Martin, his hooves clattering, and gave a loud whinny. Fauxy frantically whinnied back as she watched through the bars of the stall.

Jasmine joined Fauxy, and all three whinnied in protest as Martin led him out of the stables.

Julia and Renson had worked in the pasture with the two foals, teaching them to lead. Within sight of each other and Jasmine, they moved along with little fuss. Being led away from Jasmine and Fauxy was altogether different for Ace. Martin had a fight on his hands.

Had anyone watched him trying to get the colt home, they would have found it hilarious. Ace jumped, twisted, and reared, attempting to get loose. Martin had thick, muscular arms and broad shoulders, but Ace was a tall, strong, weanling. Even with work gloves on, Martin could feel his hands stinging as the colt yanked on the lead line. More than once, he wished he'd just loaded the colt into his horse trailer, instead.

Over and over, Ace whinnied, and spun in circles around him. Jasmine and Fauxy Lady returned his calls. Fauxy wore a path in the straw, pacing across the front of the stall.

A few times, Ace planted all four feet and refused to move forward. Martin reached around with the end of the lead and flicked it at Ace's hind end. When it touched his rump, Ace jumped forward to the end of the lead. It wasn't long before Martin felt like his arms would pop out of their sockets. Halfway home, Ace lunged forward, then reared up, too close for comfort beside the ditch. Martin's feet skidded in the loose gravel, trying to keep his footing. They both came close to falling into the ditch.

As they struggled along, a car approached, slowing to a stop across from them. Martin saw that it was Rich, a rancher from up the road. Martin tugged on Ace's lead line, asking him to halt. Instead, Ace pranced in a circle around him.

Rich rolled down the window, laughing, and said, "Looks like you've got yourself a live one, Martin!"

"Hey, Rich!" said Martin, as he wiped his brow with the back of his sleeve. "Yea, this rascal has been trying his best to yank my arms off."

"Man, oh, man, but that's a fine-looking colt you've got there!" exclaimed Rich.

"Thanks. I agree," said Martin, nodding. "But I hope he settles down. Good looks aren't everything, if they don't have a brain in their head."

They exchanged a few words, then Rich drove off slowly, careful not to spook the colt.

Even though it was a cool October morning, both Martin and Ace were soaked with sweat by the time they turned down Martin's driveway. Jasmine and Fauxy were too far away to hear Ace's whinnies, but he kept hollering. His whinnies were so loud, Martin's ears were ringing, and his arms and hands ached. The half-mile distance had taken them almost an hour.

The other horses tore to the paddock fences as Martin and Ace came into sight. They greeted the newcomer with a round of whinnies. Ace pulled on the lead line, and flipped his head up and down, trying to drag Martin over to the fence. Martin, fed up by this point, snapped the lead line a few times to get Ace's attention. At the entrance to the stables, Ace swung around and banged the door with his rump, reluctant to step inside the strange building.

Martin tugged the colt down the hall to a stall he'd prepared, earlier. He unclipped the lead, slipped out the door, and slid it shut behind him.

"Okay, buddy, you're home, as much as you don't like it, right now," said Martin, thankful that they had made it home in one piece. He leaned against the stall door and peeled off his gloves, enjoying a moment of rest.

Ace dashed around the stall, looking for an escape. More loud whinnies assaulted Martin's ears. He'd had all he could take, and headed to the house.

Once inside, he kicked off his shoes and dropped his gloves at the door. It was still morning, and he had some paperwork to do, but, for now, Martin didn't care. He washed, wrapped his sore hands around a cold beer from the fridge, then sank down onto the couch.

Weaning is a distressing time for foals, but most calm down within a day or two. Martin kept Ace in his stall for the day to let him settle.

When Julia got home from school, she listened to her dad's story, and felt worse for Ace, than for her dad. She knew what it was like to miss your mother. She went to the stables and slid Ace's stall door open a few inches. He went to Julia and gobbled the handful of chopped carrots and apples she offered him.

The next morning, Martin's hands still throbbed as he led Ace out to the round pen. Two other weanlings Martin had recently purchased were in the pen, watching with interest, as Martin unclipped the lead line. Ace barely glanced at them. He took off like a shot, his head and tail up, as he tore along the fence, looking for an escape. The other two weanlings thought it was a game, and started into the chase. Ace stopped short and whirled around, facing them. They cautiously approached each other. Breathing heavily, with his nostrils flared, Ace sniffed at them. One foal struck at Ace with a front hoof. A series of squeals, kicks, and bites ensued, but soon the three were kicking and nipping at each other, in play.

Two days later, in Renson's stable, it was Fauxy's turn to be weaned. He moved her away from Jasmine to a stall down at the far end of his stables. Although they couldn't see each other, Jasmine and Fauxy could still hear and smell each other. Renson turned Jasmine out with the other mares; but kept Fauxy in the stall for the day. She whinnied pitifully, and didn't eat her breakfast, but by suppertime, her foal feeder was empty. When Renson turned her out into a paddock the next morning with his other weanling filly, the two bonded right away.

Three weeks later, Vince arrived to brand Fauxy and the other filly. He lightly sedated them, and pressed Renson's double *RR* branding iron to their rumps. He then smoothed antibiotic salve onto their mild wounds. The brand was permanent and gave them only a slight discomfort for a brief time.

***

In the second week of December, a winter storm hit with a vengeance. High winds and heavy snow blew down from the mountains across the valley. As Julia got dressed, she looked out her bedroom window, and couldn't see the stables through the swirling snow. Two feet had fallen during the night. In the kitchen, Martin had the radio on and they listened to the news that school had cancelled classes for the day.

They knew the horses and cattle would be anxious for their breakfast, regardless of the weather. They ate a steaming bowl of oatmeal, then pulled on their coveralls and warm boots, and stepped out into the howling wind. Julia followed in Martin's footsteps as they trudged through deep snowdrifts. The snow swirled around them, stinging their faces as they leaned into the wind. As they slid the door to the stable open, a noisy commotion of hungry horses greeted them, stomping for their breakfast.

Julia and Martin started at one end of the stables, and worked their way to the other. Each horse got their ration of grain. Julia had cut some carrots and apples for Ace, which he gobbled up in his feeder. They had water buckets to fill, and hay to throw down from the loft. Martin had to shovel a path through the snow to the manure pile before he could dump the wheelbarrow. One by one, they clipped the horses onto the crossties, and gave them a light grooming.

Leaving the horses inside for the day, they closed the stable door behind them, and went back out into the storm to tend to the cattle.

By the time they headed to the house, snow had already covered their trail. Once again, Julia followed in Martin's footsteps. At the house, she shoveled the porch and walkways while Martin cleared the driveway, and made a path to the stables and cattle shed with the tractor.

They were both exhausted when they finally finished. As they hung up their snowy jackets and coveralls, they looked at each other and laughed. Their noses and cheeks were bright red from the cold.

After lunch, Julia tidied up the kitchen, then they settled in to watch a movie.

The snow and winds tapered off through the night. The plows worked overtime to clear the roads, but school was closed for the second day. By mid-morning, the sky cleared to a vivid blue. The sun glinted off the snow like shards of broken glass, so brilliant it hurt their eyes as they stumbled through snowdrifts to the stables. Julia helped Martin feed the horses. On the way to the paddocks, the horses danced with excitement, knee deep in the snow. Full of energy from being kept inside the day before, they bucked, reared, and rolled, making horse angels in the snow. With huge comical leaps, they lunged through the powdery snow, gouging deep trails through the paddocks.

Amused, Julia and Martin watched Ace's antics in his paddock. With his mane and tail flying, he pranced around, showing off to the horses in the other paddocks. He laid down to roll, then shook himself off. Covered with a fine dusting of snow, he paused, chest heaving. With puffs of steamy vapor rising from his nostrils into the icy air, he looked like a magnificent black statue.

CHAPTER SEVEN

~Springtime, Ace and Fauxy Lady~

Ace's second winter came to a close. Once again, the Beemer ranch was busy with activity. Julia and Martin were thankful when three of their mares foaled with no problems. They had bred two of them to the same black Thoroughbred stallion as Ace's sire. The mares had produced black colts, but neither had the unique marking on their faces, or Ace's sassy personality and refinement.

Julia and Martin bought a two-year-old Quarter Horse filly, and sold two yearlings. Cows were calving. They shipped some steers to auction and turned some out into the open pastures for the summer. Martin checked and repaired fences.

One morning, Martin and Julia stood at the fence after turnout, watching Ace and two yearling colts cavorting around in a paddock. They agreed that Ace had grown into an outstanding horse. He had an excellent Sport Horse temperament and conformation, and would finish out around 16 hands high. He'd lost his gangly youth, and matured into a fine looking two-year-old. They decided against having Ace gelded. He would make a magnificent breeding stallion for their mares and perhaps produce a black filly for Julia.

Martin placed a call to Vince to geld the two yearling colts. When he arrived at the stables two days later, Vince asked about Ace. "What about that orphaned colt of yours? Do you still have him?"

Martin and Julia proudly led him up the hallway to Ace's stall.

As he peered into the stall, Vince could see that even with the remains of his shaggy winter coat, Ace had grown into a stunning young horse.

Every day before turnout, Julia clipped Ace onto the crossties. First, she combed the tangles out of his long black mane and tail. Then she groomed him with a special shedding brush, to remove his itchy winter coat. His ears flicked back and forth as Julia talked to him. "Oh, you poor itchy guy!" she sighed. "When I get all this shaggy hair off, you'll be a shiny, handsome fellow."

As she worked, fine wisps of hair floated everywhere. It stuck to her face, hair, and clothes. Every day, she swept up mounds of hair from the floor. She could see she was making headway with the way his coat gleamed outside in the sunshine, but then watched with disgust as he purposely chose a mucky corner of his paddock to roll in.

***

Older colts and stallions can often be difficult and dangerous to handle. Ace had shown no aggression, so far. Unless he became unruly, Julia would continue his groundwork. She groomed him each day, then turned him out to run off some energy. When he had settled, she snapped a lead line on him and walked him in the paddock. Once a week she worked him lightly on the lunge line. He learned basic voice commands: "Whoa, Walk On, and Trot."

He acted silly sometimes, but never aggressively. Julia was patient with the colt and talked to him with a calm voice. When she fit him with a bridle, Ace accepted the gentle snaffle bit into his mouth with no objection.

Her next lesson in ground training was to introduce Ace to a surcingle. She used the surcingle as a teaching aid with two purposes, to teach Ace how to steer and halt from the ground, and to prepare him for the similar feeling of a cinch holding a saddle around his girth. The first time Julia put it on him, she turned him loose in the ring to see how he'd react. He rolled, bucked twice, and raced around for a few minutes. When Julia called him to the gate and offered a carrot, he trotted over, unfazed.

The following day, she clipped the long reins to his bridle and strung them through the rings at the top of the surcingle. She held the reins and walked behind him, teaching him to turn and halt.

Martin often watched from the sidelines, pleased with Julia's progress with the colt.

Like every young horse they raised, they would wait until Ace turned three, before anyone got on his back. Starting a two-year-old under saddle puts undue stress on the bones of a young horse. Some breeders and trainers don't agree to waiting that long.

Julia was an excellent rider, but because Ace was a stallion and could be unpredictable, they'd decided to hire a trainer to start him under saddle the following spring.

***

Fauxy Lady wasn't so fortunate. Renson didn't share Martin and Julia's reasoning to wait until a horse was three before saddle breaking them. His father had taught him long ago, that the sooner you could break a young horse, the sooner you could make a sale. That way, a rancher wouldn't waste money feeding them for an extra year.

Fauxy Lady had grown into a lovely sorrel filly with a flaxen mane and tail like her mother, Jasmine. She had Jasmine's gentle attitude and clean conformation. Not long after her second birthday, instead of turning her out into the pasture with the other horses, Renson clipped her to the crossties in the hallway. She was nervous about being kept inside by herself. Without taking time to let her sniff at it, he placed an old wool saddle pad onto her back, followed by a heavy old saddle he used for training. Fauxy turned her head and eyed the strange object on her back. With no warning, Renson yanked up on the cinch. The filly kicked out sideways with a rear leg, missing him by inches.

"Quit!" he yelled and smacked her on the rump.

As he led her to the training ring, the tight girth and weight of the saddle frightened her, and she broke into a jog. Renson roughly jerked her back to a walk. When he unclipped the lead from her halter, the young filly spun away in a panic. She lunged, bucked and rolled, trying to dislodge the heavy beast flapping on her back.

Amused, Renson scoffed as she struggled to get the saddle off, but he soon lost interest and went back to the stables to clean stalls.

Two hours later, Renson finally went to get her. She stood at the gate in misery, caked with dirt and dried sweat. Her pinched withers ached from the scratchy saddle pad and poorly fitted saddle.

When Renson yanked the saddle off, he didn't bother to brush the dirt and sweat from her coat. He just led her into her stall, tossed her a couple of flakes of hay and slid the door shut.

By the third day of Renson leaving the evil saddle on her back for hours at a time, Fauxy's withers stung with painful sores. She'd given up trying to dislodge it when he turned her loose in the paddock. Standing still was less painful than moving.

On the fourth day, Fauxy suffered another nasty experience. After he tightened the dreaded saddle, Renson jammed a fat thumb between her lips to make her open her mouth. He carelessly banged her front teeth with the heavy steel bit and roughly yanked the bridle up over her head. It was a curb bit, a severe contraption unsuitable for a young horse. She chewed on it, trying to spit it out, as he led her to the training ring.

Renson slipped the reins over her neck, then reached over and wiggled the saddle horn. That was all the warning he gave her before he stepped into the stirrup, quickly swung his leg over and sat down hard into the saddle. Terrified, Fauxy took off, bucking and twisting in circles, making a desperate attempt to get the man off her back. Her withers burned like the devil under the scratchy saddle pad. On she ran, eyes wild with pain and fear. Renson held tight to the reins. Soon the corners of her mouth were raw from the bit, as she fought to get her head. Puffing with exertion, she slid to a sudden stop. Renson, determined to ride the fight out of the filly, wouldn't let her relax for a moment to get her breath. Fauxy suffered yet another ruthless experience when he jabbed her sides with a sharp set of spurs. Fauxy shot forward in alarm, and took off at a gallop around the pen. Getting nowhere, but dizzy from circling, she slowed to a trot. The moment Renson relaxed his hold on the reins, Fauxy seized the opportunity. Her head went down and she crow-hopped around the ring, then slid to a stop at the gate.

"You are a foxy one, aren't you? I sure named you right, didn't I? Well I'm the boss, and I'll tell you when you can stop." he sneered, then raked her sides with his spurs, forcing her on. When he finally let her walk, Fauxy was lathered in sweat. Without so much as a pat on the neck, or a kind word, Renson dismounted and called it a day.

In the stables, when he pulled off the saddle, he noticed that both sides of Fauxy's withers were raw. He should have cleaned them and applied antibiotic ointment. Instead, he roughly rubbed a layer of salve on her wounds and shut the filly into her stall. She wasn't the only horse Renson had trained that ended up with raw withers. He knew the wounds would take a long time to heal, but he didn't take the time to wait.

Fauxy's wounds had barely scabbed over when Renson climbed back into the saddle two days later. She snorted with pain and made a few half-hearted attempts at dumping him. Each time she bucked, he raked her with his spurs. He roughly hauled on the reins, teaching her to turn and halt. The harsh bit rubbed the corners of her mouth raw. Although she was frightened and suffered in pain, she'd learned that it was easier to move forward and obey. Acting up just caused more pain. A week later, Renson felt proud of himself for breaking the mare so quickly. He dismounted and opened the gate.

Fauxy looked towards the stables, relieved that the painful ordeal was over for another day, but her relief was short-lived.

Renson, overly confident, decided to take her for a short ride on a trail behind his stables. He led her out of the ring, climbed back into the saddle and urged her towards the trail, away from the stables. Confused, she hesitated. Renson dug his spurs into her and she leapt forward, halted, then nervously backed up. Renson turned red with rage, and raked his spurs down her sides.

Fauxy exploded. She pitched her head down, all four feet left the ground, and she gave a mighty twist. Caught off guard, Renson's foot slipped out of the stirrup on one side, and he slid halfway out of the saddle. Off-balance, he attempted to right himself, but Fauxy seized the opportunity. She reared straight up and Renson smashed to the ground.

She turned and bolted away. The last thing Renson saw before he passed out was gravel flying from the heels of the runaway horse, pelting him in the face. As she tore away, Fauxy stepped on the dangling reins, and the bridle flew off her head.

Renson woke up, on his back, moaning. When he tried to sit up, daggers of pain shot through his lower back. Unable to get up, he knew he was in a serious predicament. He wasn't expecting any visitors, and none of his neighbors were within earshot, so he knew it was useless to yell.

He felt in his shirt pocket for his phone, cursing when he realized he'd left it in his jacket, back at the stables.

He groaned with pain as he rolled over onto his stomach, then began an agonizing crawl to the stables. Afraid he'd pass out again, he stopped every few moments, his face resting in the dirt.

Renson's other horses watched curiously from their stalls, as he crawled down the hallway, to his jacket on the floor. He felt around in the pockets until he closed his hand around his phone.

News spread quickly about Renson's accident, and the hard-luck story he told of a rattler spooking his young horse.

At the hospital, Renson lay groaning on a stretcher while he waited for surgery. The fall had fractured his tailbone and compressed the lower part of his spine. He had a long, painful recovery ahead.

Fauxy was nowhere to be found when Martin went over to Renson's that evening to feed his horses. Everyone assumed that she would make her way home within a day or two. Renson's nephew who lived in town, Martin, and another neighbor down the road, took turns caring for his horses. By the evening of the second day, the filly had still not shown up, so Martin arranged a search party. Eight people searched the trails, open pastureland, and back roads on horseback and ATVs, but there was no sign of her. Julia put up fliers, and Martin placed an ad in the local newspaper about the missing horse, but no one called.

Fauxy had disappeared into thin air.

A younger couple, who rented the apartment beside Renson's nephew, found out about his unfortunate accident. She had owned horses previously, and asked if they could live at Renson's while he recovered. Renson, facing months of rehabilitation, still flat on his back in a hospital bed, agreed. The arrangement worked out well for all of them. He let the young couple live at the ranch rent free, while they cared for his horses.

CHAPTER EIGHT

~Ace turns three~

The trainer Martin had hired to train Ace, arrived one Saturday morning in early June. Thanks to Julia's groundwork with him the previous summer, Ace already knew voice and hand commands. She'd also introduced him to a saddle and bridle. It made the trainer's job easier.

Julia and Martin watched from the rails of the round pen that first day, as the trainer walked beside Ace to loosen him up. Then he collected the reins and pressed his weight into the stirrup. Getting no adverse reaction, he stepped up and settled quietly into the saddle. Ace walked forward a few steps, then feeling the unfamiliar weight on his back, broke into a gallop, careening around the training ring. The trainer let him circle a few times to get the kinks out, then, using his voice and easing back on the reins, brought him down to a walk.

He rode Ace every day for a week, impressed at the well-behaved young stallion. The following week, the trainer urged Julia to climb on Ace's back. Julia had her misgivings about getting on, but she'd never been afraid of Ace, so she agreed to give it a try. As he walked forward, she could feel Ace's powerful muscles rippling beneath her. Even though she'd known Ace since he was a baby, and was an excellent rider, Julia was nervous. After circling the ring only once, she brought him to a halt and dismounted. The trainer agreed to ride Ace twice a week through the summer.

***

Julia graduated from high school at the end of June. The previous couple of years, during the summer, she'd taught lessons to a handful of students at the ranch, but she wanted a full-time teaching job. She placed ads in the local paper and on the internet. A few people responded, but they wanted to use their own horses in lessons. Unfortunately, the Beemer's had no extra stalls for boarders, so Julia had to find another option. She printed resumes, and using Martin's jeep, drove around to drop them off at a few larger boarding stables in the area.

A week passed before she received a call from an older woman, who introduced herself as Leigh Winters, and said that she and her husband owned Playtime Stables. The woman sounded very nice on the phone, but Julia wrinkled her brow at the name Playtime Stables. She hadn't applied there, in fact, she'd never heard of it, or Leigh Winters. Julia asked where she'd gotten her name and number. The woman told her that Cathy, Julia's former riding instructor, had passed her name on to them, and had highly recommended her as an instructor. Leigh explained that they were in a bind because they'd just been informed by their current instructor that she was taking a leave of absence. Trusting Cathy's judgement, Julia agreed to meet them, but wondered what the place was like.

A fair distance from town, Julia turned down a sun-dappled lane. She drove alongside a heavy canopy of trees on the right, and tall, evenly trimmed hedges on the left. At a gap in the hedges, a set of ornate wrought-iron gates spread open to a paved drive. She stopped, and glanced down to double-check the scrap of paper she'd scribbled the address on. When she looked back up for a street number, she noticed a sign reading, *PLAYTIME STABLES,* on a brass panel beside the gates. Her hands tightened on the steering wheel. *Whoa!* she thought as she turned in. This looked nothing like playtime, as she cruised along the winding drive, bordered by shade trees, and crisply painted white fences. Around a corner, and over a slight rise, she pulled up to the front of a white brick Victorian-style house.

Beads of moisture collected in her palms as she shifted the Jeep into park. On the way up the steps to a massive set of double front doors, she noticed a few strands of horse hair on her t-shirt, and brushed them off, then wiped her damp hands on her jeans. At the landing, she looked down in dismay at her dusty sneakers. Mounted to the right of the doors was a large brass horse-head plaque with a black button for its eye. *Is this their doorbell? You've got to be kidding me!* She pressed it. Somewhere deep inside the house she heard it chime the first few notes of the call to the Kentucky derby. *Another whoa!* Shifting from foot to foot while she waited for someone to answer, she glanced around at the manicured gardens and golf-course sized paddocks to each side of the house. The stables were nowhere in sight.

A spry-looking older gentleman with trim white hair opened the door.

Julia stammered, "H, Hi, I'm Julia."

"Hi, Julia, I'm Jack." With a warm smile, he extended his hand. "Nice to meet you. Come on in, Leigh is waiting for you."

The inside of the house was just as spectacular as the outside. Creamy marble floors gleamed, and polished antique furniture lined the foyer on both sides. Julia slipped out of her sneakers at the door and wondered if she should have worn dress pants and a blouse. *Oh, well,* she thought, *at least I have on a new t-shirt, and clean blue jeans.* In sock feet, she padded behind Jack into an office off the foyer. Seated behind a large mahogany desk, Leigh, a classy-looking woman with papery skin, gray hair in a stylish cut, and a friendly smile, leaned over the desk to shake Julia's hand. The grip of Leigh's small hand was stronger than Julia expected.

"I'll leave you two now," Jack nodded, smiled again at Julia, and pulled the door closed behind him.

"Have a seat, Julia," Leigh said warmly, gesturing towards a burgundy velvet chair. Noticing Julia's discomfort, said, "I'm not interrogating you, so just relax."

Julia perched on the edge of the velvet chair, hoping her jeans were clean enough. With the desk between them, she wiped her damp hands on her thighs.

Leigh asked Julia where she lived, then asked some horse-related questions, all of which Julia answered confidently. When she asked if Julia taught English riding, her heart sank.

"No, I took a few English lessons with Cathy. You know? The lady who gave you my name and number?" Julia raised her eyebrows, to which Leigh nodded. "But to be honest, I don't know enough to teach English lessons other than the very basics."

"That's okay," Leigh nodded and stood up. Julia was relieved to see that Leigh also wore blue jeans and a t-shirt. "Most of our students and boarders ride western, anyway. We'll figure something out for those that want English lessons. Come on, I'll show you around. We'll go out the back door to the stables."

Julia hurriedly grabbed her sneakers from the front door. At the back door, Julia noticed that Leigh wiggled her feet into a pair of well-worn, sneakers, so she felt more at ease for not wearing dressier clothes.

As the door closed behind her, Julia paused on the step, gaping at the stables across the courtyard. The outside was white brick like the house, and huge.

"Um, how many stalls do you have?"

"Forty-five." Leigh laughed, sensing Julia's apprehension. "But we have a few empty stalls. We usually have about forty students that take lessons each week. Some have their own horses, and some use our lesson horses. Our lesson schedule runs Monday, Tuesday and Thursday evenings, and Tuesday afternoons. Does that sound okay to you?"

"Yes, that sounds great."

As they entered the stables, Julia sucked in a quiet breath, and stared down the hallway. She'd never seen such spacious stalls in a stable. Everything, including the ceiling, was white-washed, with nary a cobweb in sight. Each stall had swing out water buckets and feeders. A smoky-gray, stamped concrete floor ran the full length of the hallway, without a speck of hay or manure in sight. The place was pristine.

As they strolled down the hallway, Leigh pointed out the four lesson horses. They all wore matching maroon fly sheets, except for one. Leigh pointed at the handsome bay gelding who'd come up to the bars of his stall. She explained, "Dusty destroys sheets and blankets, and just about anything else he can get his teeth on." She noticed Julia had raised her eyebrow in question at her last comment." Oh, don't worry, he's a gentleman with people. The students love him, but he can be a mischievous brat with them sometimes." She laughed, and went on to add, "he's been known to pull off saddle pads before they can get the saddle buckled up."

They proceeded down to a closed door, mid-way on the right. Leigh opened the door, and flicked on the lights to a spacious, heated, tack room. A double row of saddles and bridles lined each side, with an assortment of tack trunks below. At the far end was a kitchenette with pine cupboards across the top, a mini fridge, a sink, and a table with two chairs. To the right of the counter, she showed Julia the door to a small bathroom.

Leigh called out to Luke, who'd been mucking out a stall next to the tack room. Julia drew in her breath when he stepped into the hallway. *HOLY hunk!* He nodded with a shy, crooked grin, his dreamy blue eyes twinkling, and tipped his cowboy hat at her. He was tall, had wide shoulders, tanned muscular arms, a clean-shaven face, and his dark wavy hair peeked out from under his Stetson.

Once they were out of earshot, Leigh leaned towards Julia and whispered, "In a stable full of girls, Luke's our heartthrob around here. Oh, to be young again," and sighed.

They continued down the hallway towards a girl with her back turned, brushing a tall, Thoroughbred-type, bay horse, on crossties. A long blonde ponytail hung down the girl's back. She wore a snug-fitting hot pink t-shirt, white English breeches, tall leather boots, and a hard hat.

The girl turned her head at the sound of approaching footsteps.

"This is Liesel, and her horse, Shasta," said Leigh with a flat voice. She caught their raised eyebrows at seeing one another. "Oh, do you know each other?"

Julia cringed inside but hoped it didn't show on her face. "Yes, we went to the same school."

With barely a nod to Julia or Leigh, Liesel turned back to brushing Shasta. Liesel had been one of the snotty girls from Julia's school, and obviously her attitude hadn't changed. Julia hadn't even known Liesel liked horses. *Well*, she thought, *at least Liesel rides English, so I won't have to teach the little snoot western lessons.* As she and Leigh ducked under the crossties to pass, a flashback from high school hit Julia's nostrils. *Ugh,* Julia thought, *Liesel still wore nauseating perfume.*

Further on, Julia noticed that Leigh had gone quiet, and glanced at her. Leigh's face was flushed, her warm smile had disappeared, and her lips had flattened into a tight line. Julia assumed it had something to do with Liesel. *Not surprising*, she thought. A few teachers in high school had worn the same look when dealing with her.

Leigh noticed Julia's questioning gaze, and her smile returned, but the miniscule tightness in Leigh's jaw remained.

At the end of the hallway, Leigh slid a door open to a breezeway connected to a huge indoor arena. Windows close to the high ceilings ran along each wall to let in plenty of natural light. A few jump standards, poles, and pylons lay off to the side against a wall.

"This is just SICK!" Wide-eyed, Julia shrieked, her voice echoing through the cavernous building. "It will be so cool to teach in here when it's raining, or cold outside."

Leigh laughed at Julia's enthusiasm.

As they walked around the house back to the Jeep, Leigh asked, "Can you be here Monday evening at five? The first lesson begins at six. I'll be here, along with Luke, to help you get started. Sound good?"

"I'll be here!" Julia smiled and nodded.

She began teaching twelve hours a week. It took some time learning all her student's names. She especially loved teaching the beginners. It was fun to watch them improving each week, and learning everything they could about horses. They reminded her of herself when she was younger. Two older students confided to Julia that the previous teacher often taught while drunk. She'd been in a minor car crash after lessons one night, and had checked herself into an alcohol rehab center. *No wonder Playtime Stables needed a new instructor*, Julia thought to herself.

Leigh, impressed with Julia's patience with her students and knowledge about horses, gave Julia more hours. She not only taught, but did their books, and helped Luke muck stalls, feed, groom, and turn out horses. After a month of driving her back and forth to work, Martin bought Julia a second-hand, compact car.

Throughout the summer, Julia helped her advanced students at local horse shows. After the western classes ended, she often wandered back to the ring to watch English events. More than once, Liesel's hot-headed Thoroughbred acted up, and dumped Liesel in the dirt. As Liesel got up, her clothes disheveled, and sorely peeved at her horse, Julia had a hard time keeping a straight face.

One morning, a few months later, Julia popped her head into the stall where Luke was forking manure into a wheelbarrow.

"Good morning," she said, and was about to head to the tack room to put her purse and jacket away, when Luke called her back.

"I wouldn't go down there, if I was you," Luke said, shaking his head.

"Why, what's going on?"

"Liesel's in the tack room. Shasta's gone."

Julia's eyebrows drew together into a frown, "What do you mean Shasta's gone?"

He shrugged and said, "Her mom sold her."

Julia's eyes widened, and her hand flew to her mouth. "What? She sold Liesel's horse? Why?"

Luke just shrugged again, and said nothing.

Not heeding Luke's advice, Julia could hear Liesel's loud sobs as she pushed the tack room door open. At the table, Liesel sat slumped in a chair, with tissues pressed to her eyes. She looked up, her eyes red, and face blotchy, as Julia walked towards her past the saddles and bridles.

"Liesel, Luke told me about Shasta. I'm so sorry."

Liesel blew her nose, and followed with another round of sobs.

As much as Julia had disliked Liesel's snotty attitude, she felt terrible for the distraught girl. She bent down and wrapped her arms around her in a hug. "I'm so sorry, Liesel," she repeated. That was all Julia could offer, without knowing the facts.

"I hate her!... And I hate my dad, too!" Liesel choked out between sobs.

Julia sat across from her on the other chair, and waited for Liesel to cry herself out.

When Liesel could finally talk, there was fury in her voice. "How could I know my mother hadn't paid Shasta's board, for months? I didn't know until yesterday, that my dad lost his job in Denver, and hadn't been keeping up with his support payments." Hot tears rolled down her cheeks again, and she swiped them off with her sleeve.

Liesel got up and flipped her tack trunk open, smacking the wall behind with a thud. "Then this morning, when I asked to use her car so I could come to the stables, she told me Leigh called two days ago. We had to either pay up or find another place to keep Shasta. So, what's she do, she sells her, instead! She didn't even give me a chance to say goodbye to her!" Liesel spat out as she yanked Shasta's bridle off a hook and tossed it on top of the brushes in the trunk. "I would have tried to figure something out, but now it's too late. Shasta's gone."

Julia shook her head sadly at Liesel, not knowing what else to say. "I'll help you carry your stuff out to your car," Julia offered.

Liesel gave her a crooked smile and said, "Thanks."

After they'd loaded the bulky tack trunk, and Shasta's saddle, into the car, Julia felt terrible for the other girl. She offered, "If you want to come and ride one of our horses at the ranch, I know my dad wouldn't mind. We have a nice lesson horse that was ridden English before we got him."

"Thanks," Liesel said again, with a half-smile, surprised at Julia's generous offer. Julia picked up a hint of embarrassment in Liesel's voice, as she added, "I just might take you up on it."

***

On Julia's days off, she and Martin often saddled up two of their geldings and went on trail rides. Although it had been over a year since Fauxy disappeared, they still kept their eyes open for her. Martin suspected that she had shown up at someone's ranch, and they had quietly sold her out of state.

Fall arrived, and soon, temperatures dropped near freezing at night. Ace had done well for the trainer through the summer. They'd all been very pleased with Ace's transitions from walk, jog, and lope. Kept as a stallion, he could only have experienced riders. Every now and then, Julia got on him, but only when the trainer was around.

The horses grew thick winter coats for the coming winter. Enjoying the crisp autumn air, Ace exploded into a frenzy of bucks and kicks when Martin turned him out for exercise. Ace and the horses in the other paddocks would occasionally see bands of wild horses grazing on the ridge above the ranch. They'd whinny, and charge around their paddocks.

One afternoon, while Julia was at work, a small band of mustangs, led by a rangy buckskin stallion, ventured down the hill and approached the far end of Ace's paddock. The tough little buckskin stallion's hide bore many battle scars from defending his mares. Ace tore down the fence line towards them, his nostrils flared, tail up, and neck arched. Snorting and stamping in challenge, the two stallions touched muzzles through the fence. Ears pinned, they both reared up and struck at each other. Ace's hoof caught the top rail of the fence, and the board came loose at one end.

Martin went running from the stables when he heard the commotion. When they saw him approaching, the buckskin and his mares turned and raced off up the hill.

Ace charged around his paddock like a crazed horse. Each time Martin attempted to catch him, Ace wheeled around and tore away. He would have no part of being caught, and taken inside. Martin gave up trying to catch him, and went back to the stables to give Ace time to settle. He hadn't noticed the damage to the fence.

In an angry frenzy, lathered with sweat, Ace whinnied and charged to the end of his paddock, again. He skidded to a stop and his muzzle bumped the end of the loose rail. It swung around and dropped with a thud on the ground outside the paddock. The fence was considerably lower with the top rail down, so Ace ran in a tight circle, aimed at the fence, gathered himself at the base, and leaped out.

As he landed, red hot pain shot up into his rear hoof. A nail in the board had plunged into the tender sole. As he turned towards the ridge, the nail came out as the rail bounced away. Oblivious to the pain in his hoof, he tore up the hill after the wild herd.

Martin heard the thundering hooves, and ran back out of the stables, in time to see Ace disappear over the ridge.

CHAPTER NINE

~Ace disappears~

Martin raced back into the stables. He saddled and bridled his gelding, mounted, and kicked him into a gallop up the hill. At the top of the ridge, he reined the gelding in, quickly scanning the area. Neither Ace, nor the wild horses, were anywhere in sight. Gusty winds eliminated any chance of Martin hearing hoofbeats. Multiple cattle trails, and hoof prints, old and new, led every which way. With no specific trail to follow, Martin chose one with fresh horse manure, and urged the gelding into a lope. Over hills, past a sparse stand of trees, and through a long valley, Martin searched with no luck.

The sun would soon be down and looking for a black horse in the dark was futile. Martin turned homeward, hoping that Ace had shown up at the ranch, hungry for his supper.

It was dark by the time he arrived back at the stables. Julia heard the hoofbeats and met him outside, her face etched with concern. When she'd arrived home from work, her dad's Jeep was there, but he and his horse were gone. She'd found it puzzling that the horses were still outside in their paddocks at that late hour, and not inside for the night. As she led the first horse into the stables, her concern turned to worry, when she realized Ace's stall door was wide open, and he wasn't in his paddock.

As Martin unsaddled his gelding, he relayed the events of the day. Julia was horror-stricken to think Ace was out there somewhere in the cold, black night...

Julia placed a call to the young couple living next door at Renson's, to see if Ace had shown up there. It caught her off guard when Renson answered. He was living in town with his nephew but had dropped by, to collect some of his belongings.

He grumbled out his answer to her question, "No, he isn't here."

"Ugh, he's such a nasty man!" Julia exclaimed to her dad, as she hung up. She didn't know that her mother had shared the same opinion about Renson.

"Oh, he's just a harmless, grumpy old bachelor," replied Martin. In reality, Julia's comment was far closer to the truth.

The two of them set about calling neighbors and friends to organize a search party for the morning. Julia called Leigh to let her know what happened, that she wouldn't be in for work the next day, and to cancel her lessons the following evening.

"Take as long as you need, Julia," replied Leigh. "I'll call your students. Don't worry about a thing. Finding him is more important, and I'm sure they'll all agree."

At first light, three friends with all-terrain vehicles, and three neighbors on horseback, showed up. Julia was surprised and pleased, to see Luke, the stable hand from Playtime Stables, coming down the driveway, pulling two lesson horses in a double horse trailer. Julia's eyes widened, then narrowed as Liesel climbed out of the passenger side of his truck. She'd never taken Julia up on her offer to ride one of her school horses. Julia suspected Liesel had come only because she had the hots for Luke, and would have jumped at the opportunity to spend time alone with him. As far as Julia knew, Liesel hadn't been around Playtime Stables since the day she'd packed up and left, so Luke must have kept in contact with her. *Oh well,* Julia thought, *the more people looking for Ace, the better.* In groups of two and three, the searchers headed off in different directions.

By day's end, the weary group trickled in one by one to the Beemer ranch. None had even seen one horse, or come across any fresh signs. When Liesel dismounted, Julia overheard her whining at Luke about her sore butt, and how cold she was. *No wonder,* Julia thought, as she regarded Liesel's flimsy pink hoodie and thin riding breeches that offered no protection against the cold. Liesel hadn't worn a hat, either... *probably,* Julia mused, *because she didn't want to muss her hair.* Between Liesel whining, and most likely, shamelessly flirting with him all day, Julia could see on his face, that Luke's patience had its limits. He looked at her for sympathy, as his eyes rolled at Liesel's sniveling complaints. She overheard him tell Liesel, not so nicely, to go sit in his truck to warm up, while he loaded the horses. Before they pulled away, Julia walked over and he rolled down the window.

"Hey, thanks for coming today. I really appreciate it." She leaned in, "you too, Liesel," and nodded at her. At least Liesel hadn't worn her stinky perfume, but her lips were smeared with gaudy pink lipstick she must have just applied.

"Oh, can you do me a favor Luke?" Julia asked.

Luke nodded, "Sure. What?"

"Would you please let Leigh know that I won't be in again tomorrow morning, but tell her I'll make it for lessons tomorrow night?"

"No prob!" replied Luke. "I'd come again tomorrow too, but I just did a quick job on the stalls this morning, and didn't take the time to turn the horses out. I'm sure by tomorrow, the stalls be a complete disaster. Good luck! I hope you find him."

"Thanks Luke," replied Julia with a heavy sigh. "Me too."

As they pulled away, she bit her lower lip, and gazed at the back of the horse trailer. *Is he dating her, or what? Oh well. I don't care. None of my business.*

Liesel reached over and cranked up the tunes on the radio. Luke paid no attention. His head was turned towards his side mirror, watching Julia.

Four people showed up to search again the following day. To eliminate precious time spent scouting the same areas again, Martin spread a map on the hood of his Jeep, and pointed out the areas already covered. The group headed off, but like the first, the second day of searching proved futile.

When Julia arrived at work the next morning, Leigh and Luke were down the hallway talking. They both turned, and looked at her expectantly, hoping for good news, but the expression on her face and slumped shoulders, told them everything they needed to know.

"I just don't get it," said Leigh, shaking her head.

"I don't either, Leigh," replied Julia, with a bitter smile, "and thanks for the time off, and for letting Luke use the lesson horses to help search the other day."

"Pffft," replied Leigh, waving her off. "Don't even mention it. If I was younger, I would have gone too."

Julia went through the day with her mind in a haze. During lessons that evening, her students noticed that she wasn't her normal, bubbly, self. As the week went on, word got out about Julia's missing horse. Many of the borders and students approached her, telling her they were sorry, and that they hoped she'd find him.

On the weekend, Martin and Julia posted signs with Ace's photo and their contact information, in the windows of various businesses around town. Once more, they drove to the local newspaper office and submitted another ad, but this time for Ace, the second missing horse. Martin included a substantial reward for any information to Ace's whereabouts.

Julia posted pictures and a write-up on her social media pages. In the offhand chance someone had stolen him, she even posted ads in online classified sites that covered most of Wyoming.

A week went by. Then two.

Every chance Julia and Martin had, they saddled up and searched, but to no avail. Mysteriously, Ace, like Fauxy, had also vanished.

CHAPTER TEN

~Ace and the mustangs~

The mustangs had the advantage of knowing the trails through the hills. When Ace crested the ridge behind the paddock, he detected movement on a distant hill. Even though his hoof throbbed with pain, Ace set off at a gallop, determined to catch up.

Lathered with sweat, and feverish by the time darkness fell, Ace slowed to a walk. The night was moonless, and the stars cold and small, as he stumbled along on the rocky terrain in the dark. He wandered further and further away from the stables.

By the time the first rays of daylight arrived, Ace's hoof burned with infection, and he was desperately thirsty. He grazed on sparse grass, and rested for a brief time on a plateau, then limped on, urgently seeking water.

As darkness approached on the second night, his ears perked to the sound of rushing water, and he followed the sound. He stumbled down the rocky bank of a mountain stream, limped into the frigid water and plunged his muzzle in, sucking up great mouthfuls. The icy water was soothing on his hoof, so he remained hock-deep in the swirling stream, his body shivering with fever.

Partway through the night, a rock tumbled down the bank and splashed into the water. Ears perked towards the sound, he peered through the inky darkness where two wolves crouched at the edge of the bank, watching him. They sidled down the bank into the water. Teeth bared and snarling, the largest wolf ventured closer to Ace's front end. The other moved off to Ace's left side. Ace backed up, to keep them both in his sight.

The larger wolf gave a low growl, then boldly advanced towards Ace. Within striking distance, Ace stomped towards him. The wolf jumped back a safe distance. The smaller wolf circled to the left again.

Distracted, and unable to hear above the rushing water, Ace hadn't noticed that a third wolf approached from behind.

Ace wheeled around at a sudden stab of pain on his rear tendon. The wolf had his jaw clamped on his leg. Ace lunged forward, kicking out in fury, and the wolf lost his grip. The other two advanced towards Ace, again. Stumbling in the rocky riverbed, he turned around to face them. Seizing the opportunity of distraction, the third wolf sank his teeth into Ace's rear leg again.

Suddenly, a large, dark shape splashed through the water from upstream. The wolf yelped and released his grip on Ace, as a horse delivered a solid blow to his back. The horse bolted past Ace towards the largest wolf. The wolf turned to run downstream, but the deep water slowed him down. He howled, as huge teeth gripped his hide and shook him. The mysterious horse then turned and galloped downstream after the other wolf.

Ace, in pain, and too weak to follow, remained in the stream and listened for the return of the wolves, or the mysterious horse.

In the gray light of morning, Ace perked his ears towards a sound on a nearby ridge overlooking the river. Alarmed, he thought the wolves had returned, but up on the ridge stood the mysterious horse. Nostrils quivering, Ace caught a familiar scent. There stood Fauxy. He nickered in recognition and Fauxy nickered in return. She had saved him from the wolves!

Moments later, the wild buckskin stallion appeared at her side. The buckskin tossed his head, nipped Fauxy's flank, and urged her down the bank into the river. The stallion snorted at Ace, then took the lead upstream. Fauxy looked back at Ace, then turned to follow the buckskin.

Ace attempted to follow, but within a few steps, the pain in his hoof brought him back to a standstill.

By the afternoon, the pain in Ace's hoof was less intense, and his fever had broken. He headed upstream, in the direction Fauxy and the stallion had taken.

As he proceeded, the stream narrowed, and the banks grew steeper on both sides.

The current increased, as the stream tapered into a narrow gorge at the bottom of a towering cliff. The water was knee-deep in the gorge. The young stallion stumbled many times, pushing against the current, as he sought to find his footing in the rocky stream bed. The gorge rounded a bend towards the cliff, where it disappeared into a dark crevice. Sheer walls ran straight up on either side of the stream. Ace stopped short, uneasy at entering the gloom. He turned back, but came face to face with the wolves, struggling against the current towards him. They'd been trailing him all along.

Ace, lame and weak, had no choice. He pushed through the rushing water and entered the darkened crevice.

The wolves attempted to follow him, but the icy water was chest deep, and the current too strong to swim against. They turned back, abandoning their pursuit.

Once inside, Ace stopped and peered into the gloom, ears nervously flicking back and forth. The air was cold and dank. Rushing water echoed off the walls, preventing him from hearing the approach of danger. Only a dim light filtered down from high above, where the sheer walls opened to the sky. Jagged edges, and rocky outcroppings, created black shadows in the stream, making it difficult to see.

Ace pushed on, limping against the current. He navigated around sharp bends and brushed past rocky ledges, gouged out by years of torrential flowing water surging through the narrow chamber.

At a sharp bend, he moved to the edge of the river to squeeze past a rocky ledge that almost spanned the entire chamber. He tripped on something under the surface, but regained his footing and kept going.

Farther and farther he walked through the semi-darkness, until the river and walls brightened up ahead. Rounding a final bend, he stepped out into a sunlit valley. Towering canyon walls on both sides surrounded a meadow. A stand of trees stood at the far end of the meadow, and a crystal-clear pond ran the full length of the canyon, flowing gently towards the crevice that Ace had just emerged from.

Ace walked towards the right bank, stopping short at the sound of a branch snapping in the distance. Far down at the tree line, stood the buckskin stallion and his band of mares, including Fauxy Lady, watching him.

The buckskin gave a shrill whistle in challenge, and galloped down the shore to the water's edge across from Ace. The two horses splashed through the pond towards each other. Nose to nose, chest-deep in the icy water, they snorted and squealed at each other, necks arched, both tails aloft. The buckskin reared up, water streaming off him as he struck at Ace. Ace dodged the buckskin's hooves and slashed at the buckskin's neck with his teeth. The buckskin was smaller than Ace, but he'd fought many battles and knew all the tricks. He twisted away, then swung around and delivered a double-footed blow to Ace's chest. Ace grunted at the impact. He lunged towards the buckskin's hindquarters, but a sudden sharp pain in his injured hoof took the fight out of him. With the tender sole of his injured hoof, he'd stepped on a sharp rock on the bottom of the pond.

Painfully, Ace backed away through the water, then limped up the bank. His foot throbbing, he hobbled to the canyon wall, and found a rocky ledge to stand under.

The buckskin splashed back through the pond, triumphantly returning to his band of mares.

Although the summer grasses in the meadow had dried up, Ace found plenty of grass beneath shrubs, trees, and along the cliff wall. He kept to himself for a few days, resting under the ledge, giving his hoof time to heal. A small thicket of evergreen trees to one side of the overhang provided Ace with shelter from the wind.

He waited for darkness, to drink from the pond. The current prevented the pond from freezing across, but ice had formed along the sides. Ace broke a hole open with his hooves.

He watched the herd from afar, and he could smell Fauxy and the other mares when the wind was right.

Sometimes, at night, he heard the icy edges of the pond cracking as they left the canyon through the crevice. Ace kept to himself, and didn't follow. Before dawn, the band of horses came back through, and walked down on the opposite side of the pond to the protection of the trees at the far end.

Ace would have to face off against the buckskin stallion to win Fauxy back, and take control of the mustang mares and their weanling foals.

Each day, as the pain in his foot lessened, he became bolder. He edged closer to the pond's edge while foraging for grass, and drank during the day in full sight. The buckskin would run down to the water's edge and trumpet an angry whinny, warning Ace to stay away. Ace stood his ground, but didn't encourage a confrontation. One day, he was foraging in the center of the meadow. The buckskin went to the pond's edge, pawed the ground, and snorted a warning for Ace to back off.

Ace was ready for a showdown, this time. He plunged across the icy pond to the other side, meeting the buckskin head on. With no hesitation, they spontaneously attacked. Both reared, slashing with front hooves and biting at head, neck and shoulders. Neither would back down. The mares and weanlings kept a safe distance away on a knoll, watching the two thrashing stallions.

Ears pinned, and tails swishing in anger, they squealed, snorted, and grunted as the fight went on. Swinging around, rump to rump, they hammered at each other, hooves flying and connecting. Ace nailed the buckskin in the tendon of one leg and gashed him open. The buckskin swung around and kicked Ace in the stomach, then reared up and went for Ace's hindquarters with his teeth. The buckskin's teeth clicked together, missing his mark, when Ace lunged forward out of reach. With both hind legs, Ace kicked up, connecting on the side of the buckskin's head, near his eye. It was a solid hit, and the buckskin staggered. Ace pivoted around and kicked him square in the chest.

The older buckskin was tiring and couldn't keep up with this strong young stallion. He was beat. He trotted away, retreating down the shoreline, and out of the valley, through the crevice.

Ace trotted over to claim his band of horses.

CHAPTER ELEVEN

~Julia's search for stray heifers~

The weather turned, and it would snow, soon. It was time for Julia and Martin to round up any stray cattle still up in the hills, and herd them down to the ranch for the winter.

The area had undergone a dry spell through late summer and fall. The cattle had consumed the vast majority of decent grazing pasture nearer to the ranch. Only brittle sage grass remained, so the cattle had gradually wandered farther away, seeking more plentiful grazing.

One Saturday, mid-November, Martin and Julia bundled up in warm clothes, and packed a lunch. They saddled two geldings and headed up into the high country to search for the cattle. They would also keep watch for Ace, although they didn't hold out much hope in finding him. His disappearance puzzled them. If someone had found him, or knew of his whereabouts, they figured Martin's generous reward should have enticed people to offer information. The disappearance of Fauxy was just as baffling.

Tired and cold by the end of the day, they'd rounded up all the cattle, but two heifers. Martin had a meeting in town the following day, so Julia offered to search for them again.

"Be careful out there, Julia." Martin warned, as he collected their breakfast dishes. "Take your cell phone, and head home if you see even *one* flake of snow. Those cows aren't worth your getting lost in a storm up there. They'll either come home on their own or fend for themselves for the winter."

"Dad!" Julia exclaimed, exasperated. "I've been riding these hills since I was little! I'll be fine, and yes, I'll be careful."

The early morning sun offered no warmth as Julia zipped her jacket up to her chin, and pulled her woolen hat down over her ears. She climbed aboard the gelding and headed off in a different direction than the day before. She rode along hilltops, through valleys, and dried-up creek beds, scanning the ground for any signs of the stray cattle.

Later in the day, far from the ranch, she guided her horse down through a valley into an unfamiliar area. Discouraged, and about to turn homewards, she spotted hoofprints frozen in a mucky trail, and fresh cow droppings. She followed the trail down a bank to a shallow creek. A skim of ice formed across deep hoofprints where cattle had trod through mud near the bank.

The gelding picked his way through the shallow creek bed around rocks and boulders, and stumbled through areas of half-frozen muck. At a bend, Julia spotted the two heifers standing under a rocky shelf, near the bank of an ice-rimmed shallow pond. The pond had been their only source of water, so they hadn't ventured far.

The ice at the pond's edge snapped under the gelding's hooves, as Julia guided him into the shallow water. So as not to spook the cows, she went around them, to push them from behind. As she turned, she noticed deep grooves of multiple horse hoofprints on the muddy bank to her right, leading down to the pond. She looked to the left. Oddly, there were no hoofprints leading up the left bank. Julia tilted her head, frowning. *That's weird.*

Curiosity got the best of her, so she left the cows standing under the shelf, and urged her horse upstream. She hadn't gone far, before she realized that the stream flowed down from the direction of a sheer cliff. *Strange,* she thought. *She couldn't hear, or see, a waterfall.*

Not until she'd guided her horse around a rocky ledge, did she discover that the stream disappeared into a gap in the towering cliff. The gap ran the full height of the cliff, wider at the bottom, and narrow towards the top.

She urged her horse upstream to the opening and squinted into the gloom. In the scant light, she could see that the stream disappeared around a bend in the crevice. It was too late in the day to explore any further, and she knew she had to get the cattle home. She decided she'd go up alone the following Saturday, to explore the crevice. Knowing her dad would think it was too dangerous, she decided she wouldn't tell him about it.

It was almost dark, and the first flakes of snow drifted down, as Julia guided the wayward heifers down the hill to the cattle shed.

The next morning, Julia frowned when she pulled back her bedroom curtains. Huge flakes of snow floated past her window. She could barely make out the stables, and a thick blanket of snow covered everything in the yard. *Unless the snow melted*, she thought, *so much for going exploring next weekend.*

Martin was in the kitchen, listening to the weather station, when she wandered in to make some toast. He told her they were predicting over two feet of snowfall within the next couple of days.

"I think you should call Leigh at Playtime, and tell her you can't make it in today," Martin suggested. "Those roads will be bad out there." Julia nodded, and reached for the phone.

***

Winter had begun. Julia would have to wait until the following summer to check out the crevice. It was too dangerous to ride up there with snow on the ground.

CHAPTER TWELVE

~Julia's secret~

Mid-July, the following summer, Julia saddled her gelding and rode back up to explore the crevice. Any earlier in the summer, she knew there could still be ice and snow in the valleys and passes. Melting snow from the mountains made fast-flowing streams treacherous to cross.

Julia waited until Martin had left with a friend, to look at a stallion he was thinking of buying. She'd left a note on the kitchen table that she was going for a trail ride, packed a sandwich, saddled one of their geldings, and headed into the high country.

She knew the approximate direction of the cliffs, she just had to find the right creek that flowed from the crevice. There were so many deep ravines gouged out from the spring melt, some old, some new, they all looked alike from below. With a sinking feeling, she rode through the rough terrain, wondering if she'd find it. Finally, far in the distance, she spied the split in the cliffs. Julia guided her horse up through the next creek, and soon found the pond where the cattle had holed up the previous fall.

Julia's mount balked at the entrance to the dark crevice. He swished his tail, shook his head, and backed away through the stream. She urged him forward against the current, and allowed him time for his eyes to adjust to the dim light. With the next squeeze of her legs, he tried to turn away, but she steered him back, and applied more leg pressure. This time he stepped inside, but she could feel him quivering as he peered anxiously around, with his head up and ears perked. She stroked his neck and talked to him with a calming voice, giving him a few minutes to relax, until he realized there was no boogeyman hiding in the shadows.

They splashed through the stream, following a maze of twists and turns until they approached a rocky protrusion. It appeared to span across the entire crevice. Julia thought, *oh no, all this way for nothing*, but as they got closer, she saw a way to get around it. She guided the gelding out of the stream, into a mucky area beside the wall. The going was so narrow, Julia's knee rubbed against the edge of the rock. When her gelding stumbled on something in the muck, she looked down and her eyes widened when she saw what he'd stumbled on. There, almost buried in muck, was a saddle. She dismounted, sucking in her breath as icy water seeped into her boots. She shrugged, *oh well, I'm wet now*.

Julia pulled up on the horn, but it wouldn't budge. Using both hands, she gave the cantle a yank. In the dim light, a glint of something on the back of the cantle, caught her eye. Julia squatted down and saw a brass plate. She rubbed the dirt off with her thumb and found the initials **RR** etched into it. *RR? Hmm?* Julia tilted her head in thought, then realized the saddle belonged to Renson Reed, their neighbor. *What the heck?* Her face scrunched up, confused. *Has Renson been up here, and why was his saddle left lying in the stream?*

She remounted but had her hands full, trying to hold the gelding steady while she removed her boots, one by one, to pour out the water. As they continued, Julia kept wondering about Renson's saddle.

Further and further into the chasm they ventured, until Julia saw daylight up ahead. She felt the gelding eagerly increase his pace towards the opening.

Rounding the last bend, Julia's mouth fell open as she reined in her horse. Surrounded by towering cliffs and jagged bluffs, lay a hidden oasis, a lush meadow of grass, trees, and wildflowers. Vivid blue sky reflected off an enchanting pond that ran through the center of the meadow. Wispy spirals of mist rose from the ground on either side. Songbirds chittered and flitted from tree to tree.

Julia's mount suddenly tensed, and spooked sideways. His head high, he gazed intently towards a grove of trees at the far end of the valley. Julia followed his gaze and gasped. A jet-black horse stood at the tree line like a statue, watching her. Snorts of alarm echoed through the canyon.

Are my eyes playing tricks on me? Can this be Ace? Julia wondered.

The horse was too far away for her to see if there was white on its forehead, or if it wore a halter.

She counted seven more horses emerging from the grove of trees, one at a time. Three foals followed. They all peered nervously towards Julia and her horse.

Afraid to spook them, Julia guided the gelding slowly along the shoreline, to have a better look.

Relief flooded through Julia as Ace's distinctive white markings came into focus, but he wore no halter. It must have come off at some point.

"Hey, Ace!" Julia called across the pond. His ears flicked back and forth to the sound of her voice, and he walked down to the shoreline. The other horses warily pawed the ground, tossed their heads, and trotted around. Julia could tell from their smaller size, muscular legs, and rangy coats, they were a small band of mustang mares. As they retreated to the safety of the trees, only one remained in the open, a chestnut mare who showed no fear, and walked to stand beside Ace near the pond's edge.

Julia gasped again. She recognized the chestnut mare with the flaxen mane and tail! "Fauxy! I can't believe it! Both of you in this secret hideaway! No wonder no one could find you two."

As she sat astride her horse watching them, Julia faced a serious dilemma. Although elated to have found the two missing horses, safe and living free in a paradise, she had a decision to make. Would she tell her father of this secret place? How could Ace ever be happy back at the ranch, locked into a paddock by himself, because he was a stallion, and separated from Fauxy once again?

Julia fought with her inner demons all the way home… *do I tell him or don't I?* By the time she put the gelding into his stall and fed him, she'd decided that some day she'd tell her dad, but not right away.

She shoved her damp boots to the back of the closet when she got to the house. She didn't want them to raise any questions.

Martin had some exciting news to share. He'd made a deal with the owners of a Thoroughbred horse ranch in a nearby town. They had a well-bred four-year-old bay stallion for sale, but they were asking more than Martin had budgeted for. After a lot of discussion, they agreed that if Martin paid them half the money up front, then he could make monthly payments after that. Martin was going to trailer the stallion home the next day.

In her opinion, no other stallion could ever be as wonderful as Ace, but the more she thought about it, having a new stallion around would take his mind off Ace's disappearance. She wouldn't feel as guilty about not telling him the truth.

CHAPTER THIRTEEN

~ Fauxy's story~

Only Renson knew why Fauxy Lady had run off, and that he'd made up the story about a rattler spooking her. The gentle filly had suffered in pain until she had come to her limit. Fauxy's instinct to fight and flee kicked in.

After her escape, she'd wandered aimlessly through the hills, grazing on wild grass and drinking from mountain streams. The corners of her mouth, and the wounds on her sides from the spurs healed, but the beastly saddle was still on her back. She was itchy and the wounds on her withers burned underneath the wool saddle pad. She found a sandy area to roll, but she couldn't dislodge it. It only slipped to the side, which resulted in further discomfort for the poor horse.

A week had passed, when Fauxy perked up at the sight of horses on a distant hill. She trotted through the valley towards them.

The buckskin stallion had smelled her from afar. He was wary, and mistrusted the scent of humans, after being captured in a roundup. Wranglers had released him back to the wild, but they'd taken some of his mares and foals.

The stallion approached Fauxy cautiously, his neck arched, and nostrils flared. When he sniffed towards her hindquarters, she squealed, spun around, and struck at him. After mock posturing, with a series of squeals, charges and harmless nips at each other, the buckskin and his band of mares accepted her into the herd.

That evening, as he led his small band through the crevice towards the meadow, Fauxy's saddle horn caught on the jagged outcrop of rock. The cinch broke, and the saddle had slipped off into the stream.

CHAPTER FOURTEEN

~The following summer ~

After a long, harsh winter, Julia rode back up to the valley to check on Ace and his band of mares. She rode the same gelding, and he stepped willingly into the crevice without balking this time.

Ace was grazing alone near the pond when she emerged from the crevice. His head shot up in alarm, but when Julia called his name, he whinnied and trotted to the edge of the pond across from her. At five years old, he'd filled out into a beautiful stallion with a nicely chiseled head, long arched neck, deep chest, and powerful hindquarters. His mane and tail were long and thick, his summer coat, sleek. Julia was relieved to see he had no obvious scars or wounds. Although he was young and strong, she worried that eventually he would have to defend his mares from marauding mustang stallions.

She rode further along the shoreline, wondering where Fauxy and the other mares were. Suddenly, two small black foals came charging out of the trees, playfully nipping, and kicking at each other. Fauxy and a little bay mare followed, trying to keep up to the young ones. Julia was thrilled to see that one of the black foals, with a white star on its forehead, went to Fauxy to nurse.

More mustang mares emerged with young black foals, along with a few black yearlings. Julia smiled, assuming they were all Ace's babies. A few of the other foals had white stars on their foreheads, but from what she could see, none of them had inherited Ace's distinctive mark in the shape of a white spade.

Julia sighed with satisfaction as she headed back into the crevice. Ace, Fauxy, and the rest of the band were flourishing in the valley. It had proven to be a haven, as long as they remained there, safe from predators and wranglers.

***
~ One Morning, Late August ~

Julia was just shifting her car into reverse to head off to work, when she looked up the hill and saw a horse and foal standing on the ridge beyond the corral. Squinting against the sun, she couldn't see any details, but assumed they had escaped from one of their paddocks.

She shut her car off and ran into the stables, hurriedly grabbed a halter, lead line and a scooped a handful of grain into a bucket. As she jogged along the lane behind the cowshed, she kept glancing up to see what mare it was, but with the sun in her eyes, she couldn't tell.

Once she entered the shade of the hill, she saw it was a chestnut mare and a black foal, with a white star on its forehead. Julia tilted her head quizzically. They didn't belong to the Beemer farm, and she didn't recognize either of them. Afraid to spook them, she slowed down to a walk and talked to them in a quiet voice. The mare's head was hanging close to the ground, but she wasn't eating. As she got closer, Julia realized something was wrong. The mare's head barely moved as Julia approached. The foal's tail went up in alarm, and she scooted around behind her mother. Something about the mare looked familiar, but Julia's attention was more on her condition. Covered in sweat and trembling, the left side of the mare's head was grotesquely swollen, and her left eye was swollen completely shut.

What on earth? wondered Julia. There were no obvious cuts, or blood that Julia could see, but the mare's muzzle was two times larger than normal. Julia could hear her desperately trying to breathe through swollen nostrils. She knew the mare needed immediate medical attention.

The mare tried to walk towards Julia, but stumbled sideways. It was then Julia noticed the double *RR* brand on her rump. Julia's forehead wrinkled in confusion, but as she studied the markings on the mare's face, she was shocked when she recognized the familiar star and snip.

"Oh, Fauxy! You poor baby. What's happened to you?" she softly asked, as the mare drew another labored breath.

How did this sick mare make it all the way down from the valley, Julia wondered? *It must have taken tremendous willpower and intelligence for her to seek human help.*

Julia looped the lead line around Fauxy's neck, and urged the mare forward, one stumbling step at a time. The skittish black foal followed from a distance. Julia coaxed the mare down to the gate of the closest paddock, locked her and the foal in, and sprinted across the paddock to the stables. She grabbed the cordless phone off the base unit, and hit speed dial to Vince's number.

When he answered, Julia breathlessly said, "Hi, Vince, I hope you're not busy. I can't believe it, but Fauxy, Renson's missing mare, showed up, and she's so sick. Her head's swollen on one side, and she can hardly breathe. I don't know what's wrong, but can you come right away?"

"I'll be there in 10 minutes!" replied Vince.

***

Vince had a feeling that he knew what was wrong with the mare. He'd seen this happen many times through his years as a veterinarian. There were rattlesnakes in the area, and the snake most likely bit her while she was grazing. Most horses that get bitten by a snake receive the bite on the nose or face. When a horse sees or hears a snake, it usually lowers its head to have a closer look, and the snake strikes. Vince, like other practicing veterinarians in rattlesnake country, always kept a supply of anti-venom on hand.

"Only time will tell how this will work." said Vince after he'd given Fauxy a shot of anti-venom and a tetanus booster. "I don't know how long ago it bit her, but at least she hasn't gone into convulsions. If she hadn't shown up when she did, I doubt she would have lived until morning."

Vince showed Julia the two puncture wounds that he'd found on the side of Fauxy's muzzle.

"Lucky for her, I think it was a smaller snake. The holes of the bite aren't too far apart, which is good. I'd be a lot more concerned if those holes were wider apart. That would tell me she'd tangled with a large snake, and she'd have a lot more venom going through her system. I think she got the shot early enough that she should be fine after a few days."

Vince carefully spread Fauxy's swollen eyelid, and looked into the mare's eye with a small flashlight.

"I'm worried about her eye. It looks like she's brushed up against something because of the swelling, and couldn't see properly. I'm afraid it's done some damage to her vision on that side. I'll apply some ointment and give you some penicillin for her."

As Julia walked him to his truck, Vince shook his head and exclaimed, "Isn't that something? All this time she's been missing, and she comes back today, deathly sick, with a fine-looking filly by her side. It's like she knew you'd help her, but it's strange that she didn't go home to Renson's stables. I wonder where she's been, and who the daddy of that filly is?"

Julia just shook her head and shrugged.

After he'd left, she glanced at her watch, then called Leigh. She briefly told her the story about Fauxy and the foal, just to let her know why she was running late.

"I'm just going to check them again, then I'll be on my way in five," she promised.

CHAPTER FIFTEEN

~Fauxy and Ebony~

Martin called Renson that evening, to tell him the news about Fauxy showing up with a rattlesnake bite, and a filly by her side. Renson replied with a grunt, "Huh, isn't that something. You don't know where she's been?"

"No," Martin replied. "Not a clue. It's so strange, she just showed up on the ridge, and Julia saw her and the filly standing up there earlier today."

"Huh, isn't that something." Renson replied for the second time, then told Martin his doctor said he'd never ride again.

"I've been on pain medication ever since they discharged me from the hospital. I moved in with my nephew in town. I had to use crutches for a long time, but now, I hobble around with a cane. Big deal! I'll probably need this stupid cane for the rest of my lousy life, if I don't end up in a wheelchair. I'm on a disability pension and I don't know if you heard, but I sold my horses and put the ranch up for sale."

Martin had seen the FOR SALE sign on Renson's fence and wondered about him. He wanted to feel sorry for Renson, but he couldn't, not after seeing Fauxy's scars earlier that day, and realizing how cruel Renson must have been with her, and most likely every other horse, in Renson's stable.

As they said goodbye, Martin assured Renson they would take care of the two horses until Renson decided what he wanted to do with them.

***

It took a few days for Fauxy's swelling to go down. Her swollen muzzle prevented her from drinking from a water pail. Julia and Martin gave her water in a syringe to keep her hydrated, until she could drink on her own. The ointment Vince had given them had helped, and she ended up with just a small patch of scar tissue where the snake had bitten her.

Fauxy's withers were a different story. It disgusted Martin and Julia to see the large scars on the mare's withers. They knew the pain must have been agonizing, and that only an ill-fitting saddle would cause this kind of permanent damage. They also recognized that the thin strips of hair missing on her sides, were the result from a sharp set of spurs.

Other than being blind in one eye, Fauxy was healthy. Julia felt bad about keeping her and her filly from returning to Ace in the canyon, but Fauxy wouldn't be able to protect herself, or her foal, against predators. Besides, now Renson knew she was here, and she still hadn't told her dad about the secret canyon.

Since Fauxy's foal had never been around people, Julia began by quietly sitting in the stall to get her used to the sound and smell of her. Slowly, Julia gained her trust, and she allowed Julia to scratch her. Within days, she allowed Julia to slip on a lightweight foal halter. Soon, she had the filly walking beside her on a lead line in the paddock. Fauxy patiently followed behind the two of them.

Although the filly belonged to Renson, Julia pored over an online list of suitable horse names. She came to the name Ebony, and liked what it stood for; the strong black wood of a tree that grows in Africa.

Ebony began nickering at Julia when she walked into the stables, or approached the paddock. Every day, Julia fell more in love with the little black filly.

One day, after he finished cleaning a stall, Martin leaned on his shovel, watching Julia as she brushed the filly in the hallway.

She talked to the young horse as she worked. The filly's fine little ears flicked back and forth, listening to Julia's voice.

Martin winced, and his face took on a painful expression as he lifted his ball cap to push the damp hair off his forehead. "You know, Julia, don't get too attached to her. Renson already sold his other horses, and he'll put her and Fauxy up for sale, too," he said, in a worried voice.

"Oh, I know, Daddy," Julia brushed his words off. "Ebony rolled outside. I'm just brushing the dust off." Julia replied, attempting to sound nonchalant, but her dad's words filled her with dread.

Martin knew better. As he pushed the wheelbarrow into the next stall, he stopped dead, and his head came up with the realization Julia had just called the filly "Ebony." He shook his head. She'd even given her a name. He knew her heart would break when Renson sold the mare and foal. Martin was still making payments on the bay stallion, and just couldn't afford to buy two more horses. Renson would probably charge an outrageous price for the two of them. With the filly's impressive looks and temperament, she'd grow into a fine show horse some day, and Fauxy would make a wonderful broodmare, if she produced more foals like this one.

***

After supper one evening, Julia got up to clear the table. Martin sighed, spread his big hands on the table, and said, "Sit down, Julia."

His voice was so serious Julia felt a tingle of fear run through her. *Had Renson sold Fauxy and Ebony?* "What is it, Daddy?"

"You've been avoiding me, Julia Ann. What's going on?"

Julia's lips pressed into a thin line, her eyebrows pressed together. By the tone of his voice, and the fact that he used her second name, she knew he was really upset.

Her voice wavered, "I don't know what you mean."

"Julia, since Fauxy and that black filly showed up, you've been acting differently. It's like you've been avoiding me. What's going on? Don't try to tell me there isn't, because I know something's bothering you."

Julia looked down at the table, her stomach in knots. She looked back up at him. Her lips trembled, and tears welled up in her eyes.

"Dad, I've been keeping something from you. I know where Ace is, and where Fauxy was, before she came back," she blurted out, scared for his reaction, but relieved to tell him the secret she'd been carrying around for so long. Then she added, "I'm almost positive that Ace is the filly's father."

Martin sat back in his chair and interlaced his fingers together in his lap. He nodded and said, "I suspected Ace was her father. I also suspected that you knew something about it. So where is he, and why didn't you tell me?"

Julia told Martin the whole story from the beginning, how she found the crevice, the canyon, and the horses.

Martin sat there, stunned, listening as Julia related the story.

"Oh, Daddy, Ace is so happy up there! He's got other babies, too. Please don't make him come back here!" Julia pleaded, as tears rolled down her cheeks.

Martin didn't say a word. He sat forward at the table and pushed stray grains of rice into a small pile with his fingers. They'd fallen off his plate. He silently considered the situation. He knew he didn't want two studs in their barn. If he hadn't bought the other stallion, there would be no question about bringing Ace back home.

Julia carried the dishes to the counter. As she filled the sink, she kept glancing at her dad, wondering what he would decide, scared of his answer.

Finally, he broke his silence. "Julia, I don't like that you didn't tell me right away. I need time to think about this before I decide what to do about Ace."

As Julia wiped the table, she collected Martin's tiny pile of rice and replied in a subdued voice, "Okay, Daddy," relieved that he didn't just say no, that Ace belonged back at the ranch.

CHAPTER SIXTEEN

~Renson pays a visit~

A week later, Julia was out in the paddock with Fauxy and Ebony, when she saw an unfamiliar car come down the driveway. Martin had gone to town to get groceries. He hadn't mentioned that they were having company, or clients coming to look at a horse, so she wondered who it could be.

A shiver of fear coursed through her when she saw Renson get out of the passenger side door. Hobbling along, bent over his cane, he looked like he'd aged ten years since she'd last seen him.

Ebony followed Julia as she walked to the gate.

"Hey, Mr. Reed. How are you feeling?"

"Hi, Julia, not so great," replied Renson, gesturing at his cane. "I can barely get around anymore, but I wanted to see Fauxy, and I've heard about this filly of hers."

When Fauxy heard Renson's voice, she strode to the far side of the paddock, to get as far away as she could from the evil voice. Julia noticed her reaction, but Renson missed it, his beady eyes fastened on the filly.

Ebony, unaware that she was under Renson's scrutiny, playfully nipped at Julia's ponytail.

"Your father told me she's a beauty, and she sure is. Look at those long legs!" Renson exclaimed, as he looked the filly over. Julia's heart sank as he admired Ebony.

"I wonder where Fauxy's been all this time, and who the filly's father is? If I didn't know any better, I'd think she looks like that orphaned colt of yours, that I had in my stables. You never found him, did you?" Renson asked.

"He never came back." Julia replied, and left it at that. It wasn't exactly a lie, but she wasn't about to tell Renson the truth.

They stood and chatted for a while longer. Renson glanced one more time at the filly, then said goodbye, and limped back to his nephew's car.

After he left, Julia was relieved that Renson hadn't mentioned selling the two horses, but she was afraid the time would come.

***

After supper that night, Julia was in the kitchen doing dishes, and Martin was watching television in the living room, when the phone rang.

Julia's heart hit the floor when she heard her dad say, "Hi, Renson."

Martin walked into the kitchen with a puzzled look on his face, and said, "Yes, she's right here."

He shrugged at Julia as he handed her the phone, then went back to watch his show. He tried to listen, but he couldn't hear over the television.

Julia said goodbye, and hit the off button as she walked into the living room. Martin looked up, afraid of seeing tears, but she wore a dazed look on her face. Suddenly, she gave a whoop and shot a fist into the air.

"They're mine, Daddy! They're both mine!" said Julia, dancing around the room. "Renson is giving me Fauxy and Ebony. I can't believe it. I just can't believe it!"

Maybe Renson wasn't thinking straight because of his pain medication, or maybe he just felt guilty about Fauxy? Whatever reason that led him to give Julia the two horses, she didn't care. She just cared that they were both hers. She finally had her black filly, and Fauxy would make a wonderful brood mare for the ranch. Julia dashed out to the stables, to give Ebony and Fauxy a hug.

As she drove to work the next morning, she couldn't wait tell Leigh and Luke her exciting news. Shortly after the mare and foal had first shown up, Luke and Leigh had driven over to the

Beemer ranch, to see them. Since then, Julia had kept them updated about the mare's progress, and had raved incessantly about Ebony, so they knew how much the mare and foal meant to her.

The stable hallway was empty when she walked in. Parked in the doorway of a stall, stood a wheelbarrow piled with manure, but Luke wasn't around. As she approached the tack room, she heard voices and could smell fresh coffee. Leigh and Luke looked up from the table as she strode in. Julia was always an upbeat person, but today her face beamed. They knew something was up.

"You can't believe it, guys," and blurted out the news.

Leigh rose from her chair, and swooped Julia into her arms. "Oh, Julia! I'm so happy for you! I know how much you love them, especially Ebony."

When Leigh let go, there stood Luke, awaiting his turn. As his muscular arms pulled her close, Julia drew in the heady scent of his shaving lotion. Caught in his bear hug, she was startled at the tingle of delight that coursed through her. Her eyes widened at Leigh, who stood off to the side, her head tilted, wearing an amused look on her face. Julia felt heat creeping up into her cheeks, as he released her. She turned away, hoping Luke wouldn't notice, but when she glanced back as she went out the door, his crooked grin, and playful blue eyes, gave him away.

As she went through her day, Julia reminded herself that Luke had never shown any interest in her. Nor she, him… *well, maybe a little bit.* By day's end, she decided that she'd read him wrong, and that his hug was only to congratulate her, and nothing more.

***

A few months later, Julia had the unpleasant task of giving Leigh her two weeks, notice. She'd gone into a friend's tack shop in town, and as she browsed for a larger halter for Ebony, her friend Marcia, approached her with a proposition.

"Julia, I'm not sure if you're interested?" Marcia began, "but I need someone to take over managing this place." She shook her head, and dramatically, spread her arms. "I'm finding it so hard juggling my time between the kids and this tack shop, I'm going crazy. You know all about tack and horse supplies, and I'd go over all the ordering forms, and books with you."

Julia crossed her arms, thinking about how much she enjoyed her job at Playtime Stables.

Upon seeing doubt cross Julia's face, Marcia added, "I don't know how much you make at Playtime, but I need someone I can trust, and I'll make it worth your while."

Leigh had taken the news as well as could be expected. When Julia told Luke that she was leaving, a cloud flitted momentarily across his eyes. He held her gaze for a moment, went to say something, then changed his mind. He smiled, and wished her well, but his smile didn't quite reach his eyes.

CHAPTER SEVENTEEN

~ Ebony, springtime, four years later ~

As they knew she would, Ebony matured into a stunning four-year-old mare. She was fine-boned, with a refined head coming out of a nicely curved neck. Her delicate, well-formed ears curved inwards at the tips. When turned out, with her long legs and nicely sloped shoulders, she floated at the extended trot. Her mane and tail were long and thick. Julia worked hard to rid the mare of her shaggy winter coat. She groomed Ebony until she glistened.

Like she had with Ace, Julia had done a lot of ground training the previous year. Ebony had learned how to walk, turn, and halt, with Julia using a combination of reins and voice commands. It was time to put a saddle on the mare. Julia had bought a second-hand English saddle and a soft leather bridle with a padded noseband, and a gentle rubber D-ring snaffle.

In the round ring, Martin held Ebony's head the first time Julia mounted her. Ebony turned her head, nonplussed, and curiously looked back at Julia. When he let go, the mare just stood there. Julia told the mare to "walk on," along with a slight squeeze of her legs. She guided Ebony to the rail without so much as a swish of her tail. Not wanting the mare to get bored, Julia kept the first ride short.

They began each ride doing simple figure eights at a walk. She practiced halting and backing Ebony up. The mare willingly accepted the bit, and never tugged on the reins. With a light squeeze of Julia's calves, Ebony willingly trotted on. They made wonderful progress. After a week at the walk and trot, Julia asked her to canter. Unlike a lot of young horses starting off under saddle, the mare never attempted to buck, or act silly.

***

Martin's bay stallion had sired some beautiful foals at the Beemer ranch.

Fauxy had recently given birth to her second foal. She and her month-old bay colt grazed in the far paddock, with the other mares and foals.

One evening after work, Julia had just settled into the saddle aboard Ebony. With barely two weeks of training under saddle, the young horse's easy-going attitude had impressed Julia. So far, she'd calmly accepted everything in stride.

Julia gently nosed the toes of her boots into the stirrup irons, and reached forward to give Ebony a pat for standing still. As she collected the reins, the hair at the nape of her neck prickled, a premonition that someone was watching. She looked back towards the doorway of the stables, then to the house, but no one was around.

She shrugged off the creepy feeling, and with a light squeeze of her legs, asked the mare to walk on. Ebony suddenly tensed, spooked sideways, snorting in alarm, then pivoted on the spot and gazed up the hill behind the riding ring. *Easy, girl*, Julia spoke quietly to the trembling filly, then followed Ebony's line of sight. At the edge of the ridge stood the silhouette of a horse against the sky. Julia knew in an instant it was Ace. She wondered if the stallion had come down from the canyon to check on Fauxy and Ebony.

The stately black stallion paused for a few moments, effortlessly lifted into a jaw-dropping rear, then turned on his haunches and disappeared over the ridge. Julia heard their thundering hooves, as he and his mares galloped away.

The END

HORSE-RELATED WORDS

Bit: the metal mouth piece that is part of a bridle
Bridle: a headpiece used for steering/controlling a horse
Broodmare: a female horse used for breeding
Colt: a male horse under four years old
Filly: a female horse under four years old
Foal: a baby horse, male or female
Gallop: the fastest movement of a horse
Gelding: a male horse that has been castrated
Halter: a headpiece worn by a horse
Heifer: a young cow before she has had her first calf
Jog: a slow, two-beat diagonal gait of a horse
Lope: a slow, controlled gallop
Mane: the longer hair that runs down along the top of a horse's neck
Mare: a female horse over four years old
Stallion: a male horse over four years old
Stud: an uncastrated horse (stallion) used for breeding
Surcingle: a training tool that secures around a horse's girth
Tack: a bridle, saddle and other equipment worn by a riding horse
Weanling: an older foal that no longer drinks its mother's milk
Withers: the bony bump at the bottom of the mane where it meets the horse's back. The front of a saddle sits at the withers.
Yearling: a one-year old horse

ACKNOWLEDGMENTS

With love and gratitude, thank you:

To my father, the late John Vincent, the day you lifted me as a toddler onto the back of a horse, you sparked the flame to my life-long love of horses. I know in my heart you would have been my greatest fan through my years of showing horses. You also taught me my love of reading, and savoring the suspense and drama of a good book.

To my mother, who loved animals, and taught me to treat them with respect and kindness. You were the rock of our family.

To my husband Tom, who has always supported his horse-crazy wife, and for the many evenings you watched television alone, while I pounded away at my keyboard writing this story.

To my sons Robin and Curtis, my daughter in law Julie, and my two grandchildren Olivia and Nora, I thank you for your love, support, and encouragement.

To my three non-horsey brothers, who endured many trail rides when we were young, accompanying their horse-crazy little sister, every time my birthday rolled around.

To my dear friends, who cheered me on, through the years that I showed horses, and through the writing of this book. Your love, support, and encouragement will always be appreciated.

To Amy Maltman, another dear friend of mine, fellow horse-lover, and fellow author, you've helped and encouraged me along my journey in writing my first book.

To my beta readers, Sam Ramsay, Amy Maltman, and Tom Feifel, I appreciate every suggestion and correction.

To my skilled editor, Kathleen Rothenberger, I appreciate your expertise in catching, and correcting my mistakes, and for helping me to produce a successful story.

SAVE AND PROTECT THE WILD HORSES OF NORTH AMERICA

In my story, Julia finds out about the devastating, and often fatal, occurrences, during wild horse round-ups. Although my story is fictional, the terror and horrors these horses experience during the round-ups, is anything but fictional.

I only wish that all the wild horses and burros could find safe, secret hideaways like Ace and his band, where they can live in peace, wild and free.

***

Every little girl should know a horse's love, and every horse should have their own little girl. Those of us that have known that love, are never complete without a horse in their lives.

A quote, by fellow horse-lover, Candy Jacomella-Blas

ABOUT THE AUTHOR

This is Ann's first novel.
Ann Feifel lives in northern Ontario with her husband, and two spoiled little dogs. She has been a horse and animal lover her whole life. She is a proud mother of two sons and a daughter- in-law, and cherishes her two granddaughters. They are a family of animal lovers, both domestic and wild.

Animals have always been an important part of Ann's life. She has owned horses, a pony, a goat, a handful of beloved dogs, and a rescue cat.

A former employee at the local S.P.C.A., Ann assisted many lost, homeless, and injured animals. She supports Hope for Paws, a non-profit animal rescue organization, and speaks out against mistreatment and cruelty to animals.

A NOTE FROM THE AUTHOR:

If you enjoyed reading ACE, please leave me a rating (1-5 star) and I'd appreciate it if you'd write a few words on the review page of Amazon or Goodreads.com **To find the review page on Amazon**, scroll way down on Ace's book page to where it says, *"Review this Product"* Click on that "very difficult to see" button that says *"**Write a Customer Review**."*
On the Goodreads page, type Ace the Black Stallion into the search bar, then click on the review button once you arrive at my book page.
The sequel to ACE, **SAVING SNOW DRAGON**, will be available on Amazon October 2022

Thanks so much, and have a great day, people! Ann Feifel

Made in the USA
Las Vegas, NV
08 May 2024

89668512R00089